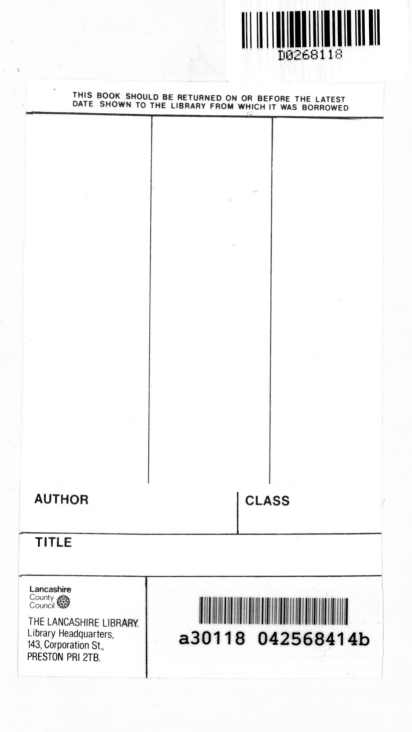

THE GIOCONDA SMILE

A Play in Three Acts

From the Short Story
by
ALDOUS HUXLEY

Samuel French – London
New York – Sydney – Toronto – Hollywood

THE GIOCONDA SMILE

Produced at the New Theatre, London, on the 3rd June 1948, with the following cast of characters—

(in the order of their appearance)

HENRY HUTTON	*Clive Brook*
JANET SPENCE	*Pamela Brown*
NURSE BRADDOCK	*Mary Merrall*
CLARA	*Pamela White*
DORIS MEAD	*Brenda Bruce*
DR LIBBARD	*Noel Howlett*
GENERAL SPENCE	*Gordon McLeod*
MAID	*Elizabeth Villars*
1st WARDER	*Kenneth Law*
2ND WARDER	*Allen Montgomery*

SYNOPSIS OF SCENES

ACT I

SCENE 1   The living-room in the Huttons' country house. Lunch time. A day early in May

SCENE 2   The same. Midnight, the same day

ACT II

SCENE 1   The same. Evening. June

SCENE 2   The same. Afternoon. July

ACT III

SCENE 1   The living-room in the Spences' cottage. Afternoon. October

SCENE 2   A prison cell. The following afternoon

SCENE 3   The living-room in the Spences' cottage. Late the following night

SCENE 4   The prison cell. The same night

SCENE 5   The living-room in the Spences' cottage. Early the next morning

THE GIOCONDA SMILE

ACT I

SCENE I

SCENE—*The living-room in the Huttons' country house. A day early in May.*

The room is Regency but has had an extra pair of large french windows added to it. Both pairs of windows, one up C and the other R, open on to a verandah and give a view of the garden. There are double doors up L leading to the entrance hall, staircase and other parts of the house. The fireplace, in which stands an electric radiator, is down L. Below the french windows R there is an alcove in which stands an easel and a pile of canvases. The room is comfortably and well furnished. Well filled, built-in bookshelves flank the fireplace. Library steps stand against those above the fireplace. A large cabinet, with a display of silverware on top, stands between the doors and the french windows up C. There is a writing table R, between the two pairs of windows. A small circular dining table stands RC with two upright chairs, one L of it and one R of it, and an armchair above it. The sofa, which is LC, has small occasional tables R and L of it. There is an easy chair down L, with an occasional table L of it. A low upholstered stool below the sofa completes the furniture. On the walls hang a number of post-impressionist French paintings; a Braque, a Matisse, a Derain and a Picasso. The windows are beautifully curtained, and the floor is carpeted. There is a table-lamp on the writing-table, and a telephone and table-lamp on the table L of the sofa.

(See the Ground Plan at the end of the Play)

When the CURTAIN *rises, the table RC is set for lunch, which has reached the dessert course, and a trolley, above the sofa, has sundry dishes upon it. The double doors are shut and both pairs of french windows are open.* HENRY HUTTON *is seated in the armchair above the table RC. He is about forty-five, handsome, full of charm and a good talker.* JANET SPENCE *is seated R of the table. She is about thirty-five, very well-bred, very much a lady, but a little too intense in manner to be an altogether comfortable companion. A third place is set L of the table.*

HUTTON (*picking up the decanter*) A little more?

JANET. Just a drop.

(HUTTON *pours some wine into Janet's glass and replaces the decanter. As he does so,* NURSE BRADDOCK *enters up L. She is a large and rather formidable woman in her middle forties, dressed in a white overall and nurse's veil*)

1

HUTTON (*to the Nurse*) Well, did she eat her chicken?

NURSE (*moving to the trolley*) Just a few mouthfuls that's all. It's one of our bad days, I'm afraid. (*She helps herself to stewed fruit*) And the noise these workmen are making in the house doesn't help your wife.

HUTTON. My dear Nurse Braddock, dry rot in houses, as in people, must be eradicated at the source. (*To Janet*) Incidentally, the workmen are threatening to invade this part of the house next month, so I shall probably have to entertain in the shrubbery. I must come over to your house one evening, and have a game of chess with your father.

JANET. He'd love it. Oh, that reminds me, we're in the most awful fix; father's nurse has just told us she wants to leave.

(*The* NURSE *moves to the table with her plate*)

HUTTON (*picking up the decanter*) Who? That nice pretty young thing? (*He offers wine to the Nurse*)

NURSE (*shaking her head*) No, not for me, thank you. (*She sits* L *of the table*)

HUTTON. Sorry, I'd forgotten. Strictly teetotal. People with no small vices terrify me. Like the devil, they reserve all their energies for the really big things.

JANET. She's getting married. I don't know what we're going to do.

NURSE. Getting married? I thought she had more sense than that.

JANET. You don't happen to know of anyone who could take her place, do you?

NURSE. Not for a paralysis case. We don't much care for paralysis cases as a rule. But I tell you what I'll do, Miss Spence. I'm going out this afternoon. I'll drop in and talk to the sister in charge.

JANET. That's really very kind of you.

NURSE. Not at all. It's a real pleasure. Oh, and by the way, Mr Hutton, I hope you don't mind if I'm not back till late. Mrs Hutton said she didn't have any objection.

HUTTON. So why ask me? (*He indicates the Nurse's glass of water*) And I trust you won't be brought home drunk and disorderly. (*To* JANET) I must show you my new picture after lunch.

JANET. Another one? Henry, aren't you ashamed of yourself?

HUTTON. I simply couldn't resist it. An early Modigliani. One of these extraordinary nudes.

JANET. I'd love to see it.

HUTTON. You must help me decide where to hang it. You too, Nurse.

NURSE. Don't hang it anywhere—that's *my* advice.

JANET. Don't you like it, Nurse?

NURSE. Like it? It makes me absolutely sick.

HUTTON. From which, my dear Janet, you can infer that it must be pretty good. Only the very best modern paintings make Nurse sick. The second-rate things don't cause anything worse than a touch of heartburn.

NURSE. Mrs Hutton didn't like it either. In fact, she . . .

HUTTON (*interrupting*) She thought it was positively disgusting. I knew that without your telling me.

NURSE (*rising with dignity*) If you'll excuse me, Miss Spence, I'll go and take some dessert up to the poor invalid. (*She moves to the trolley and proceeds to fill a plate with stewed red-currants*)

HUTTON. You're not going to give her those red-currants, are you?

NURSE. Why not?

HUTTON. Remember what Dr Libbard said. Nothing with skins or pips.

NURSE. I believe in letting her have what she fancies. It does her more good than fussing around with diets and things.

HUTTON. All right, have it your own way; but don't blame me if it upsets her.

(*The* NURSE *picks up the plate she has filled and exits up* L)

If only somebody would marry this one instead of yours. But that, I fear, is a lost cause.

JANET. Poor thing!

HUTTON. And yet Emily fairly dotes on the woman. So here she is, for life—poisoning every meal I eat. There are two ways of being a martyr to ill-health. The first way is to suffer from it. The second is to suffer from the sufferers. I sometimes wish I could try the first way for a change.

JANET. To listen to you, one would think you were a monster. Luckily your friends know better.

HUTTON. Do they? Well, it's more than I do. All *I* know is that I'm not St Francis of Assisi. Nothing would induce me to kiss the leper. And, fortunately, I'm rich enough to pay other people to do it for me.

JANET. Why are you so cynical, Henry?

HUTTON. Because I enjoy the pleasures of an easy conscience. Cynicism is simply confession without repentance. You admit your sins, and so you get rid of the unpleasant necessity of concealment and hypocrisy; but, having confessed, you neither repent nor reform. You advertise your shortcomings and you persist in them.

JANET. What nonsense you talk, Henry! Everybody knows how patient and kind you've always been.

HUTTON (*rising*) In other words, what a very adequate income I've always had. (*He moves to the table* R *of the sofa and takes a cigar from the box on it*)

JANET. Darling Emily—you know how devoted I am to her.

But even I have to admit—well, she doesn't make life too easy for the people around her. Or for herself, if it comes to that.

HUTTON (*cutting the end of his cigar*) She's her own worst enemy, of course. But then, who isn't his own worst enemy? (*He lights his cigar*)

JANET (*after a pause*). I often wonder what I'd do, if I were ill and lonely and felt that nobody really cared for me. I think I'd commit suicide.

HUTTON (*easing* L *of the table* RC) One doesn't commit suicide because one has a reason for killing oneself. One does it because —well, because that's how one's mind happens to work. I've known lots of people whose life was obviously not worth living; and yet the idea of putting an end to it never even entered their heads.

JANET. But if you knew that, because of your life, other people's lives weren't worth living, wouldn't that make a difference?

HUTTON. Not a bit of it. It would probably make you hold on even tighter—just to annoy your friends. Some people kill themselves out of spite; and some refrain from killing themselves, also out of spite. On the surface, the symptoms are slightly different; but at bottom it's always the same disease.

JANET. Well, I hope that if ever I felt I was in the way, I'd have the strength of mind to get rid of myself.

HUTTON. You'd have the strength of mind now, when it isn't necessary. But if you ever *were* in the way, you'd only have the strength of mind to sit tight.

JANET. Don't make a joke of it, Henry.

HUTTON. I'm not making a joke; I'm trying to tell the dismal truth.

JANET (*rising*) You don't believe I'd have the courage? (*She eases to the window* R)

HUTTON. It isn't a question of courage. It's just a matter of physiological reactions. (*He sits on the sofa*)

JANET. If I couldn't do it myself, I'd ask someone else to do it for me.

HUTTON. No, you wouldn't. Not at that stage of the proceedings.

(CLARA, *the maid, carrying a tray with coffee, enters up* L, *moves down* L *of the sofa, and puts the tray on the stool*)

Good, here's the coffee.

(CLARA *moves up* L, *then to the cabinet up* C)

JANET. I'd ask them in advance, while my judgement was still good. I'd make them promise that, if ever I came to be a burden, they'd do what I ought to do myself.

HUTTON. Dear Janet, you're incorrigibly high-minded. Like the noblest Roman of them all.

(Clara *looks in the cabinet up* c)

What is it, Clara?

Clara. Mrs Hutton wanted her smelling salts.

Hutton. Is she feeling faint?

Clara. No, sir, I don't think so. She just wanted her smelling salts.

(Clara *finds the smelling salts, moves to the trolley and pushing it ahead of her, exits with it up* l)

Hutton. "She just wanted her smelling salts." (*He sighs and shakes his head*) Sometimes I just want to go to Patagonia and never come back.

(*There is a long pause*)

(*He rises*) Well, let's have coffee.

Janet (*moving to the stool*) Let me do that, Henry. I'm very impatient to see the new picture.

Hutton. You are enthusiastic. All right. (*He moves to the alcove down* r) You deal with the coffee. I'll get the easel out right away. (*He draws the easel out a little into the room*)

(Janet, *with her back to the audience, pours out four cups of coffee*)

Janet. Emily takes sugar, doesn't she?

Hutton (*moving to the alcove*) Yes, give her a lot. (*He selects one of the pile of canvases and places it on the easel*) She likes something to take away the taste of her medicine.

Janet (*placing a cup of coffee on the table* r *of the sofa*) I've put an extra lump in the saucer.

Hutton (*standing back and looking at the picture on the easel*) There. (*He moves* c *and picks up the cup of coffee from the table* r *of the sofa*)

Janet. No, that's Emily's cup. It's too sweet for you. (*She hands him a second cup of coffee*)

(Hutton *places the second cup of coffee on the table* r *of the sofa.* Janet *picks up her own coffee, crosses and looks at the picture on the easel*)

Hutton. I'll take it up to her.

Janet (*looking at the picture*) Exquisite.

(*The* Nurse *enters up* l. *She has taken off her overall, and is wearing a frock and hat. She carries her coat and gloves, and a small tray with a medicine bottle and glass on it*)

Well, how's your patient, Nurse?

Nurse (*moving above the sofa*) Oh, as well as you can expect, all things considered. (*She puts her coat and gloves on the back of the sofa*) I'll take up the coffee at once, if you don't mind. I want to catch the two-forty-five bus.

HUTTON (*moving above the* R *end of the sofa*) Don't you bother, Nurse. I'll do this. (*He takes the tray from her*)

NURSE. No, really, that's quite unnecessary.

HUTTON. Drink your own coffee. (*He indicates the coffee tray*) You've just got time. (*He puts the first cup of coffee on the medicine tray*)

NURSE (*moving* L *of the sofa and then to the stool; grudgingly*) Well, that's very kind of you, I'm sure. (*She picks up the remaining cup of coffee*)

HUTTON (*moving to the doors up* L) And don't make yourself sick by looking at that.

(HUTTON *points to the easel, turns and exits with the tray up* L)

NURSE. That poor Mrs Hutton.

(JANET *starts and turns*)

I feel so terribly sorry for her.

JANET (*moving below the table* RC) Yes, with a heart in that condition, I suppose she might go at any moment. (*She drinks her coffee and places the cup on the table* RC)

NURSE. It isn't her health I'm thinking about. It's—well, you know. (*She pauses while she drinks her coffee*) Miss Spence, I could tell you things that would make your hair stand on end. (*She puts her cup on the coffee tray and moves* C)

JANET. What sort of things?

NURSE. The sort of things you find out, if you've been nursing for twenty-three years. In the best families, what's more. When I think of that poor angel upstairs there . . .

JANET. When I first knew her, she was a beauty. Had her pictures in the papers, and all that sort of thing. Then came her illness. Suddenly there was nothing left to her. None of the things that had made her life worth living. No parties, no theatres, no admirers, nobody to court her and flatter her, nobody even to listen to her.

NURSE. Isn't that typical of men? Sex—that's all *they* care about. Nothing but sex. I wouldn't trust any of them. Not even the Archbishop of Canterbury. Did Mrs Hutton ever talk to you about—you know? (*She glances toward the door*)

JANET. No. What does she say?

NURSE (*moving above the sofa*) Just like all the rest. Sex—that was the only thing *she* ever meant to him. And when that was finished—well, good-bye. It's a wonder he hasn't gone off with someone else. (*She picks up her coat from the sofa and puts it on*)

JANET. He wouldn't do that. He's too loyal.

NURSE. You mean, he knows which side his bread is buttered. Look at the money she's got.

JANET. That's got nothing to do with it. He's a rich man. He doesn't depend on her money.

NURSE. The richer people are, the more they value money

That's what I've always found. And in any case when a man's rich, he can get all the sex he wants just by paying for it. No scandal, no divorce; money, that's all.

JANET. Does Mrs Hutton suspect . . .? I mean, does she think there's another woman?

NURSE. Oh, he's clever enough to keep things dark. But, I tell you, we wouldn't be surprised at anything.

JANET. Mrs Hutton and you seem to have talked things over a great deal.

NURSE. Now, dear, you mustn't feel jealous. (*She perches herself on the R arm of the sofa*) There's nobody she cares for more than you. She's told me that again and again. But, after all, you're not a registered nurse; you're not even married. She'd feel embarrassed talking to you. Whereas, I'm like the doctor. You don't mind taking off your clothes for the doctor, do you? Well, that's how she feels about talking to me. And then, though I say it as shouldn't, she likes me, she feels I'm a friend. I'll tell you something. Do you remember that brooch of hers—that diamond dragonfly?

JANET. Yes, I know the one you mean.

NURSE. Well, she's going to leave that to me in her will.

JANET. Oh, I'm so glad. That means she cares for you—and poor Emily has so few people to care for.

NURSE. And so few who care for her, Miss Spence. (*She puts on her gloves*) Well, I must fly, if I'm going to catch my bus. (*She rises and moves to the window up C*)

JANET. And if you should hear of somebody who can look after my father . . .

NURSE. Don't worry, dear. We'll find someone for you. (*She bends down and picks up a large tin that was on the veranda and looks at the label*) That idiot of a gardener. If I've told him once I've told him a hundred times. Imagine leaving this stuff for the weeds about where the dogs can get at it. Just like a man. The stupid dolt. Sometimes I think it would be a good thing to abolish the entire male sex. We'd do much better without them.

(*The* NURSE *exits up* C *to* L, *taking the tin with her.*
    JANET *stands motionless for a few moments then moves to the chair* L *of the table* RC, *and sits facing the picture on the easel. She studies it for a few moments, then* HUTTON *enters up* L)

HUTTON (*moving behind Janet's chair*) Well, what do you think of it?

JANET. It's really lovely.

HUTTON. And to think he might still be alive and painting these things. I have no patience with these people who die young. All these Keatses and Shelleys and Schuberts—it's just idiotic. Make a note of it, Janet; you're invited to lunch on my eightieth birthday.

JANET. You're sure you won't be a bit bored with me by then?

HUTTON. No. I'll still be wondering what's going on behind that mysterious little smile of yours. What *is* going on, by the way? (*He moves and sits in the armchair above the table*)

(JANET *smiles at him without speaking*)

Or is nothing going on? You know how wonderfully spiritual a dog can look. Like the soul's awakening. And then suddenly it starts hunting for fleas.

JANET. You think that's the sort of person I am?

HUTTON. I wish I could. It's so restful when women are like that. What you do is what Modigliani does.

JANET. How do you mean?

HUTTON. Look at this figure. Perfectly flat. And yet all the modelling's there. It's the line. If the line's good enough, it implies the volume. You know there's a third dimension. Well, some people are like that. They're flat; they don't say anything in particular; they make no obvious effort to express themselves. And yet you're aware of depths and volumes and psychological spaces. Well, you're one of those people.

JANET. I don't know whether to be flattered or offended.

HUTTON. Both and neither. It's a wonderful thing to have a rich personality. But if you have a rich personality you cannot fail to include a good number of quirks and oddities—not to mention the other things, the shameful things, the reptiles in the basement, the black beetles behind the wainscot.

JANET. And that's me, is it?

HUTTON (*rising*) That's you, my mysterious Gioconda. (*He moves down* R *to the easel*)

JANET. This reminds me of the first time I ever saw a post-impressionist painting.

HUTTON. When was that?

JANET. "When was that?" (*She shakes her head*) That just shows how little we can communicate with one another. We're each on our own little island. You wave to me; I wave to you. But we can never land on anyone else's island, never find out how he lives, what he thinks and feels.

HUTTON. Perhaps that's something we should be grateful for. I know I'd be horribly embarrassed if anyone came ashore and started exploring. (*He sits* R *of the table*)

JANET. And yet it's terrible to realize one's isolation. For example, something happens to you, something enormously important and significant. And yet, for the person who was with you when it happened, the person who was the cause of its happening, it doesn't mean anything at all. Do you remember a young woman who came back from India?

HUTTON. A very charming and beautiful young woman.

JANET. That's neither here nor there. The point is that you

showed her your pictures; you took the trouble to explain to her what they were all about.

Hutton. Ah, I begin to remember.

Janet. But *she* never forgot—that's the difference. Do you know what you did for me, Henry? You opened a door, and there were all the things I'd only heard about—painting, criticism, music. It was like a revelation, like a conversion. And you didn't feel anything of what I felt.

Hutton. How could I? After all, I hadn't spent some of the best years of my life in an Indian garrison town.

Janet. And to think that, but for you and the grace of God, I might be there now. A colonel's lady—that's what I'd be by this time.

Hutton. And who knows? Perhaps you'd be very happy, my dear. Perhaps you made a great mistake when you turned down your nice young captain.

Janet. Henry, how can you say that?

Hutton (*rising*) After all, a man can have very bad taste in art (*he looks at the pictures*) and yet be a very good husband. And vice versa, I may add.

Janet. But the one doesn't *necessarily* exclude the other.

Hutton. No, I've known people who could make the best of both worlds. Such as a certain person who likes this sort of thing. (*He indicates the painting on the easel*) How happy I'd be if I had someone who'd look after me as devotedly as you look after your father.

Janet. You talk as though I were a monster of altruism.

(Hutton *draws the easel with the picture on it into the alcove down* r)

Hutton. I'm sorry, my dear—you are. But in spite of it, you can look at this without being made to feel absolutely sick, like Nurse or poor Emily. (*He eases below the table* rc)

Janet (*rising*) How strange that Emily never learned to care for painting. (*She moves to the sofa and sits at the* l *end of it*)

Hutton. Oh, but she does. She cares a great deal. But her taste isn't very catholic. She likes portraits, and only portraits of herself, and then only if they're flattering and by very expensive painters.

(Clara, *pushing the trolley, enters up* l)

Clara. Excuse me, sir, Mrs Hutton says, would you please come upstairs for a minute.

Hutton. Tell her I'll come later on.

Clara. She wants you to come now, sir.

Hutton (*crossing to the door up* l) Oh, very well, very well. Sorry, Janet. I won't be long.

Janet. I'll have to be going in a moment, anyhow.

HUTTON (*turning*) But wait till I come back. Please.
JANET. Of course.

(HUTTON *exits up* L.

CLARA *proceeds to collect the coffee tray, cups, etc. and to clear the lunch table, putting the things on the trolley. She turns the armchair above the table* RC *to face the writing-table*)

Clara, is Mrs Hutton feeling worse?
CLARA. Not that I know of, miss. And, anyhow, worse or better, it doesn't make much difference.
JANET. It must be hard work for you with an invalid in the house.
CLARA. Oh, you get used to it, miss. You get used to anything.
JANET. Until the moment comes—when you say, that's enough.
CLARA. And a lot of good that does you. Because, when you come down to it, one thing's just as bad as another. That is, if it isn't worse. You may have invalids here; but if you go somewhere else, it'll be drink, or stinginess, or carrying on with actresses, or Roman Catholics, or pet monkeys. You can change your job as much as you like—there's always something wrong. So stay where you are. That's *my* advice.

(CLARA *pushes the trolley to the doors up* L *and exits with it.*

JANET *rises, moves to the library steps, mounts them and selects a book from the shelves above the fireplace. As she does so,* DORIS MEAD *tiptoes across the verandah and peers in the window down* R. *She is twenty-two and provocatively pretty. For the moment she does not notice* JANET, *who hears her and turns*)

JANET. What are you doing here?
DORIS (*startled*) Oh!
JANET. Are you looking for somebody?
DORIS. Yes—Mr Hutton.
JANET (*descending the steps*) Was he expecting you?
DORIS (*stepping into the room*) Well, not exactly. But, I mean—he knows who I am.
JANET. Why didn't you ring at the front door?
DORIS. I—I came through the garden. It was shorter. J mean . . .

(*The door up* L *is flung open and* HUTTON *enters*)

HUTTON (*as he enters*) Well, it was nothing, of course. Just fuss for fuss's sake. (*He catches sight of Doris and a look of startled apprehension appears on his face. Then he readjusts his expression, smiles politely, crosses and shakes hands with her*) Miss Mead. What a pleasant surprise. I don't think you know Miss Spence. (*He turns to Janet*) Miss Mead is collecting subscriptions for the Crippled

Children's Homes. (*To Doris*) I've got the cheque ready for you, Miss Mead.

Doris. Oh—thank you.

Hutton. The only thing is that I'd like to earmark the money for spastics. (*He moves to the writing-table and picks up some papers*) I couldn't quite make out what form I had to fill up. (*To Janet*) Excuse me, won't you?

Janet. I'll say good-bye, Henry.

Hutton. No, no. (*He replaces the papers*) I won't be a moment.

Janet. But I've got to go. Thank Emily for me, and tell her how sorry I am I couldn't see her. (*She puts the book on the back of the sofa*)

Hutton (*moving to the doors up L*) I will. (*He opens the door*)

Janet. No, don't bother. I'll find my way out. Good-bye, Miss Mead.

Doris. Good-bye. (*She crosses below the table RC*)

Hutton. I'll ring up tomorrow and see what we can settle about that game of chess with your father.

Janet. Yes, do that.

(Janet *exits up* L.

Hutton *closes the door, turns and moves to Doris with an angry expression*)

Hutton. You little idiot.

Doris. Oh, darling. (*She tries to put her arms around Hutton's neck*)

Hutton (*pushing her away*) No, no, none of that. I'm very angry with you. You know quite well you've no business to come here.

Doris. I know, darling. But I was with Lily Peters in her car, and when we passed the gate I just couldn't resist it.

Hutton. And you see what happened? It's lucky I had those papers lying there.

Doris. You were wonderful, Teddy Bear. Crippled Children . . . (*She laughs*)

Hutton. There's nothing to giggle about. If you got the spanking you deserve, *you'd* be a crippled child. (*He gives her a sound smack on the behind*) Go and sit down before anything worse happens to you.

(Doris *crosses to the stool and sits. She looks around the room. Her eye comes to rest on a large picture by Matisse, representing several blank-faced and distorted nudes, squatting or reclining in the midst of gaudily patterned draperies, near a table and vase of flowers that seem to lean forward*)

Doris (*pointing*) Goodness! What's that?

Hutton. Rather nice, isn't it?

Doris. But, Teddy Bear—— (*She looks at Hutton, sees that he appears to be perfectly serious; then looks back at the picture*) But—girls *aren't* like that. I mean, you wouldn't like it if I . . . (*She breaks off in embarrassment*)

(HUTTON *laughs, sits* R *of her on the stool and puts his left arm around her*)

HUTTON. No, I certainly wouldn't. But, fortunately, you're not a piece of canvas.

(DORIS *nestles close to him.* HUTTON'S *desires get the better of his annoyance. He kisses her once, draws back, then kisses her again with a kind of ferocity.* DORIS *goes limp in his arms. When he next draws back she opens her eyes*)

DORIS. You look like an owl.
HUTTON. I won't say what *you* look like. It wouldn't pass the censor.
DORIS. You beast. (*She thumps him*)

(HUTTON *catches her wrist, brings her hand to his mouth and bites it*)

Ow, you're hurting me.
HUTTON. Good. (*He bites her hand again*) Cannibalism.

(DORIS *withdraws her hand, and her face assumes a serious expression*)

DORIS. Darling, do you love me?
HUTTON. Like a cannibal.
DORIS. No, this isn't a joke. I mean, do you *really* love me?
HUTTON. Do I *really* love you? Well, I must first know what your definition of reality is. Are you an empiricist? Do you believe exclusively in concrete particulars—such as this ear, that absurd little nose, this delicious mouth? (*He touches Doris's ear, nose and mouth as he names them*) Or, on the other hand, are you a Platonic idealist? Do you believe that Love with a large L exists before any particular love with a little "l"? In other words, do you regard concepts as prior to percepts?
DORIS (*rising*) Stop it. I hate it when you talk nonsense. (*She perches herself on the* L *arm of the sofa*)
HUTTON. Sorry, my pet; I thought I was talking metaphysics.
DORIS. I know you don't really love me. But I don't care. I can love enough for two.
HUTTON (*rising*) What about having dinner with me tonight?
DORIS (*rising*) Oh, that would be wonderful. (*She sits* C *on the sofa*)
HUTTON. Good. (*He sits on the sofa* R *of her*) But, now you've got to promise me something. Never come to this house again. It's pointless, it's idiotic and it's dangerous. So, you mustn't.
DORIS. All right, I promise. (*She pauses*) Tell me, is—is *she* in the house?

HUTTON. Who do you mean?

DORIS. You know quite well who I mean. Is she still so ill?

HUTTON. Let's talk about something else.

DORIS. I know—I'm not fit to mention her.

HUTTON. Don't talk nonsense. It's simply a question of tact, of good taste.

DORIS. In other words, you're ashamed. You don't want to be reminded of what you're doing—you just want to do it and not think about it.

HUTTON. Exactly.

DORIS. And do you know what that means? It means you don't really care for me. *I'm* not ashamed. I wouldn't mind telling everybody. Because I love you, because I feel this is the best thing I've ever done. You certainly don't feel that.

HUTTON (*with a wry smile*) No, one doesn't feel too proud of—well, of being a seducer.

DORIS. I like that. Do you remember the first time you kissed me? Well, I'd made up my mind beforehand that I was going to make you kiss me. And I did make you.

HUTTON. Well, I'm damned!

DORIS. So, you see, you needn't feel so guilty. But I won't talk about her. I know it makes you miserable. And, besides, I'm dreadfully sorry for her really. *And* for you, if it comes to that.

HUTTON. Why for me?

DORIS. Because you can't be as happy as I am. (*She pauses*) The one who was here just now—was that *Janet* Spence?

HUTTON. Yes.

DORIS. I didn't imagine she was like that—not from the way you've talked about her. Why, she's as old as the hills.

HUTTON. Well, of course, from your point of view she's practically got one foot in the grave. To me, she looks like a very attractive girl of thirty-five. She used to be really lovely ten years ago.

DORIS. And I suppose you flirted with her?

HUTTON. Naturally. (*He picks up the book off the back of the sofa*)

DORIS. Do you still flirt with her?

HUTTON (*rising and moving to the bookshelves above the fireplace*) Only in the most spiritual way. We do a sort of Dante and Beatrice act. (*He replaces the book on the shelves*) You know—soul mates. (*He turns*) What's the matter?

DORIS. Sometimes I really hate you.

HUTTON (*moving above the sofa*) But, luckily, you have your own inimitable way of showing it. Don't be silly. Can't you understand a joke?

DORIS. It isn't a joke. You *do* care for her.

HUTTON. I don't care for her. I just care for the things she cares about. She's the only person in this god-forsaken neighbourhood who isn't a barbarian or a Philistine. What about a little drive this afternoon?

DORIS. Oh, that'll be lovely.

HUTTON. Where to? Ivinghoe Beacon?

DORIS. Yes. Do you remember those butterflies we saw there last time? Like sparks of blue fire. And afterwards on the scabious flowers—opening and shutting their wings. Blue, blue—and then underneath, it was like silver freckles. Let's go, Teddy Bear.

HUTTON (*moving to the doors up* L) All right, I'll go and get my things and tell them I shan't be in this evening.

(HUTTON *exits up* L.
DORIS *rises, moves* R *and studies the pictures on the easel.* HUTTON *re-enters up* L)

Well, I've established my alibi; you'll be glad to hear that I'm dining with old Mr Johnson to discuss the war memorial. (*He moves* C *and fills his cigar-case from the box on the table* R *of the sofa*) At the present rate of progress it'll be ready just in time for the next little massacre to end all massacres. Or even the next but one. That is, if there's anything left of us by then. (*He moves to Doris and takes her arm*) Meanwhile, my pet,

"The grave's a fine and private place,
But none, I think, do there embrace."

From which we can draw only one conclusion.

DORIS. What's that?

HUTTON (*leading her to the window* L) Don't waste time talking.

(*They exit* L)

CURTAIN

SCENE 2

SCENE—*The same. Midnight. The same day.*

When the CURTAIN *rises, the room is in darkness. The doors up* L *are closed. The windows are closed, but the curtains have not been drawn and there is faint moonlight outside. The table from* RC *and the upright chair from* L *of it have been removed.*
(*See the Ground Plan at the end of the Play*)

DR LIBBARD *is dozing on the sofa. He is in his late fifties, quiet and slow spoken.* HUTTON *enters through the french windows up* C, *moves to the table* L *of the sofa, switches on the table-lamp and sees Libbard.*

HUTTON. Doctor; Doctor, what are you doing here? Is my wife ill?

LIBBARD. Hutton, I've been waiting for you for four hours.

The servants tried to reach you at Mr Johnson's. But they had no news of you there.

HUTTON. No, I was detained. I—I had a breakdown.

LIBBARD. Your wife kept asking to see you.

HUTTON (*moving to the doors up* L) I'll go up to her at once.

LIBBARD. I'm afraid it's too late.

HUTTON (*turning*) Too late? (*He looks at his watch*) Yes, I suppose she's asleep. (*He moves down* L)

LIBBARD (*rising*) I'm afraid not. Emily had a heart attack about four hours ago.

HUTTON. Dead?

LIBBARD. Yes. Unfortunately, I was out when they called me. I didn't get here till it was all over.

(HUTTON *turns away*)

It was the Nurse's day out, too. The only person who was with her, except for the maids, was Janet.

HUTTON. Oh, they sent for Janet, did they?

LIBBARD. I think her presence must have been a great comfort to poor Emily. These heart attacks—they give you such an awful sense of apprehension. Sheer animal panic. It's a great help to be able to hold somebody's hand, to feel you're not completely abandoned.

HUTTON. It's strange; she hadn't been complaining of her heart these last days.

LIBBARD. It came on suddenly. There was a violent attack of nausea in the afternoon. That was the thing that knocked out the heart. I understand from the maid that she'd eaten some red-currants at lunch.

HUTTON (*turning*) Do you mean to say *that* could have killed her?

LIBBARD (*sitting on the sofa*) Indirectly, yes. When a heart's in the condition hers was in, you can't risk the smallest indiscretion. The cause is trivial, but the consequences may be disastrous.

(*The* NURSE, *wearing her outdoor clothes, enters up* L)

NURSE (*moving* C) Oh, excuse me. I saw a light in here and I wondered . . . Oh, Dr Libbard—is anything wrong?

HUTTON (*bitterly*) Nothing—except that you've managed to kill your patient.

NURSE. What do you mean?

LIBBARD (*rising*) Mrs Hutton died of heart failure while you were out.

HUTTON. And it was because you let her have those currants. Do you remember?

LIBBARD. Is this true, Nurse?

NURSE. But she—she liked them so.

Libbard. You know how strongly I've always insisted on a bland diet.

Nurse (*moving up* R) I didn't think that a few currants . . .

Libbard. That's enough, Nurse. You went against my instructions. You were absolutely in the wrong. Admit it.

(*The* Nurse *starts to cry*)

Hutton (*crossing to* c) I warned you at the time, but you insisted on taking them to her. You wanted to have your own way, didn't you? Admit it.

(*The* Nurse *sits in the armchair* L *of the writing-table.*
Janet *enters up* L)

Libbard. Please, Hutton. This is a professional matter.

Janet. Henry. (*She moves to Hutton, takes his hands in both of hers and stands for several seconds in silence*) She looks so calm now, so beautiful. You feel she's come home at last; come home and gone to sleep.

Hutton. I think I'll go up to her room.

(Hutton *crosses to the door up* L *and exits.*
Janet *moves and puts an arm about the Nurse's shoulders*)

Janet. I know it must have come as a terrible shock to you. You were so devoted to her.

Nurse (*brokenly*) Dr Libbard says it was my fault.

Janet (*turning to Libbard*) Her fault?

Libbard. I gave certain instructions; Nurse Braddock chose to ignore them. Whether this was actually responsible for what happened tonight, I can't say. But, it most certainly might have been. Currants are about the last thing I'd have allowed Mrs Hutton to eat.

Janet. You think it was the currants?

Libbard. She didn't eat anything else that could have upset her like this. You'd better go to bed, Nurse. There's no point in your sitting up any longer. You can't do anything for anyone.

(*The* Nurse *rises and, still holding her handkerchief to her face, crosses and exits up* L)

Janet (*easing* c) What are you going to do about this, Dr Libbard?

Libbard (*sitting on the stool*) I suppose I ought to report her to her organization. The odd thing is that she's really a first-rate nurse. Careful, conscientious, never silly or absent-minded—and, yet, here she does something that's absolutely inexcusable. I don't understand it.

Janet. I think I know why she did it.

Libbard. I suppose she cared too much for her patient— thought she was doing the poor woman a favour.

Janet (*moving above the sofa*) Yes, she really loved Emily. But, that's only part of the explanation. The other part is that she wanted to spite Henry.

LIBBARD. Why?

JANET (*moving* L *of the sofa to the fireplace*) She didn't like him, that's all.

LIBBARD. Just because he belongs to the male sex, I suppose. Some of them get like that.

JANET. Henry was always very keen on Emily's sticking to her diet. That was enough to make Nurse Braddock ridicule the whole thing.

LIBBARD. With the result that she kills the person she's most attached to. (*He sighs*) Oh dear!

JANET. She must be feeling the shock more than any of us; I'd like to help her if it's possible. You know my father's nurse is leaving us.

LIBBARD. My poor Janet.

JANET. I was thinking I'd ask Nurse Braddock to come and take her place. That is, if you feel she'd be all right.

LIBBARD. Well, as I've said, she's an uncommonly good nurse. And I don't think there'd be any psychological difficulties, would there?

JANET. No, I think she likes me quite well.

LIBBARD. And the General's an old man, and paralysed into the bargain. So, I don't see why she should feel any subconscious resentment against him.

JANET (*perching herself on the arm of the easy chair down* L) The only thing is that, if you were going to report her . . .

LIBBARD. Well, I'd hate to ruin the poor woman's career.

JANET. Do you think there'd be any danger of her making this kind of mistake with us?

LIBBARD. No, I don't. (*He pauses*) All right. I won't say anything on condition she goes to you. I'll still be in touch with her in that case. (*He rises and moves* C)

JANET. I think you're very generous.

LIBBARD (*turning*) One just tries to use a little discrimination, that's all.

JANET (*rising*) Should I go and talk to her, do you think?

LIBBARD. Do. The poor woman was obviously in an awful state. I'll wait here for Hutton. (*He sits on the sofa at the* L *end of it*)

JANET (*moving to the doors up* L) Very well.

(JANET *exits up* L.
    After a few moments HUTTON *enters up* L)

LIBBARD. Well, there's nothing to say, of course. Just a lot of platitudes that don't signify anything.

HUTTON (*moving* C) Have a drink, Libbard?

LIBBARD. No, thanks. One talks in one universe; one dies and one suffers in another. I found that out when Margaret died.

HUTTON. You two were very close, weren't you?

LIBBARD. We'd been married nearly thirty years.

HUTTON (*moving to the writing-table*) Thirty years. And yet it isn't the time that counts. It's what you feel, and what you are. (*He switches on the lamp on the writing-table and picks up a framed photograph*) Do you remember Emily as she was then?

LIBBARD. Margaret used to say she was like the princess in a fairy story.

HUTTON (*reading an inscription on the photograph*) "To my darling—wilt thou sail with me?"

LIBBARD. Shelley?

HUTTON. Yes, he wrote it to an Emily too. (*He quotes*)

"Emily,
A ship is floating in the harbour now,
A wind is blowing o'er the mountain's brow;
The merry mariners are bold and free:
Say, my heart's sister, wilt thou sail with me?"

And we did sail. We even landed on Shelley's enchanted island. (*He moves to the window R*)

"Our breath shall intermit, our bosoms bound
And our veins beat together, and our lips,
With other eloquence than words eclipse
The soul that burns between them . . ."

We used to read it together. (*He pauses and turns*) Shall I tell you where I was this evening?

LIBBARD. I don't think you need. It seems sufficiently obvious.

HUTTON (*moving c; the photograph still in his hand*) I suppose you think I'm pretty contemptible, don't you?

LIBBARD. I don't think I have any right to pass that kind of judgement.

HUTTON. Well, I do. That's what I am, that's what I've always been—contemptible.

LIBBARD. I've never thought so. But I've felt extremely sorry for you sometimes.

HUTTON. Ugh! (*He turns, moves to the writing-table and replaces the photograph*) Contemptible—no goodness, no order, no sense or meaning—just futility, squalor—squalor. The moral equivalent of a slum. That's what my life has been and in an obscure kind of way I've always known it; but I wouldn't face the fact.

LIBBARD. You've had nothing to make you face the fact.

HUTTON (*sitting in the chair down R*) Perhaps not. But I was capable of being—I won't say a better man, because that's claiming too much—but I was capable of achieving—achieving *something*.

LIBBARD. Being born with a lot of money as you were—it's no joke. God knows it's dreary enough to earn one's own living;

but at least it gives a certain purpose and direction to one's existence.

HUTTON. And if you're rich and haven't to earn your living?

LIBBARD. If you're rich you can afford to live discontinuously, without identifying yourself with any purpose larger than your own beastly little cravings. And, in the last analysis, that's not being quite human.

HUTTON. Do you think I'm capable of changing?

LIBBARD. Of course—if you want to.

HUTTON. I *do* want to.

LIBBARD. At this moment, yes. But, it's so easy to be heroic in time of crisis. What's difficult is to behave even moderately well at ordinary times. At this moment you could do anything. Will you feel the same a month from now?

HUTTON. Do you think I'm as weak as all that?

LIBBARD (*rising and moving* C) How should I know? It wouldn't surprise me if you were. And it wouldn't surprise me if you weren't. At fifty-eight I've stopped being surprised at anything.

HUTTON (*rising*) I see. (*He moves to the writing-table, sits and prepares to write a letter*)

LIBBARD. What are you doing?

HUTTON (*writing*) Just one moment.

(LIBBARD *moves out on to the verandah by the window* C *and looks up at the sky*)

LIBBARD (*turning in the window*) The moon's almost full. What I hated most when I worked in London was never seeing the sky —only a lot of smoke, with whisky advertisements. (*He re-enters the room as he continues to talk*) That's what makes modern man so idiotically bumptious. He lives in a horrible little home-made universe and thinks he's conquered the God-made one. He's industrialized himself to the point where he's in danger of exhausting all his natural resources. Wasting assets—that's what our whole civilization's based on. A few of us are rich because modern man has chosen to get rid of his irreplaceable capital in the shortest possible time.

(HUTTON *seals up his letter, stamps it and turns to Libbard*)

And Emily was one of that lucky minority. She could buy or hire everything our civilization has to offer. And I've seldom known anyone more unhappy than that poor woman was. Or more restricted, more shut in, less free, in spite of all her liberty of choice and movement. And now she's dead. (*He moves below the sofa*) And that's what progress has done for her. (*He picks up his bag from the sofa*) Well, I must go. I've got a heavy day in front of me tomorrow. (*He moves* R *of the sofa*)

HUTTON (*rising*) Drop this in the letter-box as you go by, will you? (*He hands Libbard the letter he has just written*)

LIBBARD (*taking the letter*) I'll try not to forget.

HUTTON. No, don't. It's important.

LIBBARD (*reading the address on the envelope*) "Miss Doris Mead." I can't believe that anyone called Doris can be as important as all that.

HUTTON. Very important to say good-bye to.

LIBBARD. Oh, I see. Then I certainly shan't forget. (*He puts the letter in his pocket*)

HUTTON. You're quite right: one doesn't know what one will be thinking and feeling a month from now—so let's do the irrevocable today. Then one can't change one's mind tomorrow.

LIBBARD. You're growing wise in your old age. (*He moves up* LC) Good-bye, Hutton. I'll look in tomorrow.

HUTTON. Good-bye, Libbard; and thank you for all you've done for me.

(JANET *enters up* L.
    HUTTON *turns and moves to the window* R)

LIBBARD. Well, what news?

JANET (*crossing to* C *and turning*) She's very grateful to you, Dr Libbard.

LIBBARD. And you'll have a new nurse, I hope?

JANET. As soon as Henry will let her go.

HUTTON. The sooner the better, as far as I'm concerned.

LIBBARD. Good-bye, Janet.

JANET. Good-bye.

(LIBBARD *exits up* L.
    JANET *moves down* C)

HUTTON. I'm so thankful you were with poor Emily at the end. Did she—did she suffer much?

(JANET *looks at him for a moment without speaking; then suddenly turns away and, covering her face, begins to sob uncontrollably*)

(*He moves to her*) Janet. (*He lays a hand on her shoulder*) Don't let's talk about it any more. It's been too much for you.

JANET (*between her sobs*) It was terrible; it was so terrible. I'd never seen anybody die before. I didn't realize . . . (*She breaks off and hides her face against his coat*)

HUTTON. Try to think of her only as she is now. She's at peace. The agony's over. You mustn't think of that.

(*There is a pause, then* JANET *raises her head*)

JANET (*turning and moving to the fireplace*) I just can't keep the memory away. It's like an obsession—I suddenly see her, struggling for breath. With that awful look of pain and fear on her face. (*She shudders*)

HUTTON. Yes, but you must remember all those years of suffering and unhappiness—and now she's free.

JANET (*turning*) Yes, free.

QUICK CURTAIN

ACT II

SCENE 1

SCENE—*The same. Evening. June.*

Some of the furniture has been moved and is covered with dust sheets. Stepladders, tins of paint, brushes and other equipment indicate that the room is in process of being redecorated. The writing-table is now down R, with the easy chair L of it, and the stool is down RC. The sofa has been pushed further L. The occasional table from L of the sofa, with its lamp and telephone, is against the bookshelves above the fireplace. The library steps are in front of the window up C. Two upright chairs remain, one up RC, and the other down L. The armchair and the occasional table from R of the sofa have been removed. The painters' stepladders are L, between the windows.

(See the Ground Plan at the end of the Play)

When the CURTAIN *rises the stage is empty. The doors up L are half open. The windows are closed and the curtains are partially drawn, but sufficiently open to show the effects of an early twilight due to a threatening storm. The room is in comparative darkness and the telephone is ringing. After a few moments,* HUTTON, *wearing a raincoat, and carrying a suitcase, enters up L, puts the suitcase down, and lifts the telephone receiver.*

HUTTON (*into the telephone*) Oh, you've got them, have you? (*He switches on the table-lamp*) I say, you have been busy . . . Have you got a double room for tonight? A nice double room . . . Yes, with a bath—a nice double bath . . . The name is Hutton; Mr and Mrs Henry Hutton . . . I don't expect to be in before ten-thirty. (*He replaces the receiver, picks up the suitcase, places it R of the stool, takes off his raincoat, and puts it on the writing-table. He then turns back the dust sheet a little, takes some papers from off the writing-table, moves to the stool down RC, sits, opens the suitcase, looks through the papers, and starts to put them in the suitcase*)

(JANET *raps on the window up* C)

(*He rises and turns*) Who's there? Janet! (*He thrusts the papers in his pocket, moves to the window up* C *and stumbles over the library steps*) Damn these workmen! (*He draws the curtains aside and opens the window*)

(JANET *enters*)

(*He closes the window, leaving the curtains open*) What a pleasant surprise!

JANET (*moving* L *of the easy chair* R)   I'm the one to be surprised.
I thought you were in Cornwall.

HUTTON (*moving down* C)   So did I, until this morning. I had to
go to town unexpectedly. So, I thought I'd take the opportunity
to do a little burglary on the way.

JANET. Without telling us you'd be here?

HUTTON. My dear, I simply didn't have the time to let you
know. It was all decided in such a hurry. Besides I'm just driving
through, post-haste. How on earth did you know I was here?

JANET. We decided to walk down to the village after dinner.
And then suddenly I noticed a light in the house.

HUTTON. But you can't see the house from the road.

JANET. We were on the footpath.

HUTTON. Oh, the footpath.

JANET. So I let father and Nurse Braddock go on and climbed
over the fence.

HUTTON. More burglary. Well, I'm delighted. (*He uncovers the
sofa*) This seems to be relatively free of dust. Sit down, won't you.

JANET. May I? I won't stay long. (*She sits on the sofa*) Only till
the others get back from the village.

HUTTON (*moving to the writing-table*)   I hope they won't get
caught in the rain. It looked pretty menacing just now. I'm glad
you came, Janet. It'll save me writing a letter and going to the
post office. (*He takes a bracelet from the drawer of the writing-table*)
Don't look. (*He crosses to Janet and puts the bracelet on her right wrist*)

JANET. What's this?

HUTTON. There.

JANET. But, Henry, it's—it's Emily's bracelet.

HUTTON. And Emily would want you to wear it.

JANET. Me?

HUTTON. I don't know anyone who has as much right to it as
you do. Her best friend; the person who did more for her than
any other.

JANET. Henry, I couldn't. I—I don't deserve it. (*Greatly
agitated, she tries to undo the bracelet*)

HUTTON. Well, who else does, if you don't?

JANET (*holding out her hand*)   Take it off, please.

HUTTON. But, Janet, she loved you. She'd want you to have
something that would always remind you of her. And, you were
very fond of her, weren't you?

JANET. No, Henry, I can't.

HUTTON (*taking hold of her hand*)   Janet, I shall be offended, if
you won't take it.

(*There is a pause*)

JANET. Do *you* want me to have it?

HUTTON. Of course I want you to have it.

JANET. I just felt it was too much.

HUTTON. Too much? (*He shakes his head*) Not nearly enough.

(JANET *gives Hutton one of her smiles, then looks down at the bracelet*)

JANET. It's really very beautiful.
HUTTON. Do you mind if I finish off this little job, while we talk? (*He indicates the suitcase and takes the papers from his pocket*)
JANET. Of course not.

(HUTTON *sits on the stool, glances quickly at the papers and puts them in the suitcase. There is a sound of distant thunder*)

HUTTON. Did you hear that? (*He glances over his shoulder at the window up* c) It's as black as pitch.
JANET. How much longer are you going to be away, Henry?

(*There is a flash of lightning*)

HUTTON (*rising*)   Don't ask me. Ask the workmen. (*He moves to the writing-table and collects some more papers*)
JANET. I suppose you'll be back in two or three weeks?
HUTTON (*non-committally*)   Thereabouts. (*He puts the papers in the suitcase*) Perhaps a little longer. Various things have turned up recently.

(JANET *rises*)

I may have to be in town for a bit.

(*There is a louder peal of thunder*)

What about your father and the nurse? They're going to get awfully wet, aren't they? (*He sits on the downstage arm of the easy chair*)
JANET. Oh, they'll take shelter somewhere. (*She moves to the window up* c *and looks out*) I love thunderstorms, don't you? (*She mounts the library steps at the window*)

(*There is a flash of lightning*)

HUTTON. Frankly, I don't. I once saw a man killed by lightning. Just a few feet away from me.

(*There is a heavy roll of thunder*)

It wasn't funny. Goodness, this is like the overture to *William Tell*.
JANET (*peering out*)   Look at the trees. Writhing, struggling. As if they were trying to get free. But they can't, they're tied down.

(*There is a flash of lightning*)

The wind blows through them, and all it can do is to torture them, tear them to pieces, destroy them.

(*There is a roll of thunder, rain starts to fall, and the lights all go out*)

Hutton (*rising*) I knew this would happen. (*He gropes his way towards the door up* l *and bumps into the sofa*) Damnation!

Janet. Where are you going, Henry?

Hutton. To get a lamp.

Janet. Oh, don't. You can see the lightning better as it is.

Hutton. I'm not interested in seeing the lightning.

(Hutton *exits up* l. *There is another flash of lightning*)

Janet (*counting*) One, two, three . . .

(*There is a peal of thunder as* Hutton, *carrying an unlighted hurricane lamp, enters up* l *and crosses to the writing-table*)

It was less than a mile away that time.

Hutton (*fumbling under the dust sheet on the writing-table*) I can't find the matches.

(*The rain commences to fall in torrents*)

Janet. Listen. (*Ecstatically*) What a release!

Hutton. Here we are. Thank goodness. (*He takes the lamp and matches to the stool* rc)

Janet. It's like somebody who's had to keep everything locked up inside herself—and then suddenly she can let go. You must know what that's like, Henry.

Hutton (*lighting the lamp*) Know what what's like? (*He leaves the lamp on the stool*)

Janet. Having to hide the thing that's most important to you; being forced to live a lie. Against your will, against all your feelings.

(*There is a flash of lightning*)

Hutton. This is getting too close for my taste.

(*There is a peal of thunder*)

Janet (*descending the steps*) You can't be happy, if you're living a lie.

Hutton. Can't you? I don't know. (*He sits on the downstage arm of the easy chair*)

Janet. But how could you be under those conditions? And, after all, everyone's got a right to happiness.

Hutton. A right? Why should it be a right? I don't claim anything by right. I just take what happens to come my way and thank my lucky stars.

Janet (*moving down* c) Poor Henry. You haven't had much happiness in your life, have you?

Hutton. Oh, I don't complain. I've done pretty well, all

things considered. Health, money, books, pictures, not to mention friends and even . . .

(*There is a flash of lightning, followed almost immediately by a thunderclap*)

Golly, how I hate this. (*He laughs*) You're quite right, I'm far from happy at this moment.

JANET. You can make a joke of it. But, I know what you've been through, Henry. The isolation. The spiritual loneliness. I've known what that can be. You're surrounded by people, but you live in a vacuum. There's nobody to understand or sympathize, nobody you can talk to about your most precious thoughts and feelings.

HUTTON (*sympathetically*) Yes, your poor father—it must have been pretty difficult sometimes.

JANET (*nodding*) So, you see, I realize what you've had to go through. Darling Emily. So sweet and kind, and with that touching, childlike quality. But, she was no companion for a man like you, she could never share in your tastes and interests. She could only . . .

(*JANET is interrupted by an almost simultaneous flash of lightning and clap of thunder*)

HUTTON (*wincing*) It's right overhead.

JANET. It's wonderful. It's like—it's like passion.

HUTTON. Now, Janet, you've been reading too many novels. Passion, passion . . .

JANET. But you know what I mean. Loving so much, or hating so much, that at last it breaks out, in spite of yourself. Like lightning, like a thunderbolt, like the wind and the rain.

(*There is a flash of lightning*)

HUTTON. And woe to the man who hasn't got an umbrella.

(*There is a peal of thunder*)

JANET. Henry, we're free now. We needn't pretend any longer.

HUTTON. Pretend what?

JANET. I tried to hide it; but you must always have known, Henry. Just as I always knew about you.

HUTTON. About me?

JANET. Yes, of course. I knew what you felt, and I knew you'd never admit it—out of a sense of honour and duty. I admired you for that, Henry, even though I suffered from it. Those little jokes you used to hide behind. And then, how careful I always had to be, never to talk about ourselves, only about books and pictures and music. Good acting—but we always knew what lay behind it. And now there's no more need for acting. It's been so long, Henry. And I cared so much.

HUTTON. But, Janet, listen to me. It's impossible.

(*There is a flash of lightning*)

JANET (*moving in to Hutton*) But, Henry, you've forgotten. We can do what we want now. There's nothing to prevent it any more. We don't have to think of anyone but ourselves.

HUTTON. Janet. There's something you don't understand. (*He rises and moves up* C)

(*There is a more distant peal of thunder*)

JANET. I'm sorry, Henry.

HUTTON (*looking through the window up* C) My dear, don't let's say anything more about it. You're overwrought. It's the thunder.

JANET (*sitting on the downstage arm of the easy chair*) I ought to have known how you'd feel about it. It's still too recent, too painful. Poor Emily . . .

HUTTON (*turning*) Emily?

(*The rain eases*)

JANET. That face—I thought I'd put it out of my mind. So frightened, so horribly frightened. And I talked about—about us. No wonder it upset you.

HUTTON (*turning and looking out of the window up* C) The storm seems to be moving away. It isn't raining quite so hard. Do you think we ought to take the car and see if we can rescue your father? (*He moves down* C)

JANET (*ignoring his question*) Henry, this won't make any difference later on, will it?

HUTTON. In what way?

JANET. When the pain has worn off, when we can think of ourselves again.

HUTTON (*moving to the sofa*) Oh, I see what you mean. (*He hesitates, in embarrassed uncertainty; then makes a plunge*) Listen, Janet, I think I ought to tell you. (*He sits on the sofa*) While I was away in Cornwall . . .

JANET. What happened while you were in Cornwall?

HUTTON. Well, to cut a long story short, I got married.

(*The rain ceases*)

JANET. You got married?

HUTTON (*with forced nonchalance*) It's someone you don't know. As a matter of fact, *I*'ve only known her for a few months. I'm sure you'll like her when you meet her. Of course she *is* rather young—only about twenty-two, as a matter of fact. Quite a baby.

JANET. Twenty-two?

HUTTON. So, you see, she has plenty of time to learn. And

she'll adapt herself soon enough. Young people seem to be so
sensible nowadays, so much on the spot. Very different from
what we were at their age.

(JANET *suddenly breaks out into a peal of violently mirthless
laughter*)

(*He looks at her apprehensively*) What are you laughing at?
JANET. Oh, nothing in particular.

(*The electric light comes on again*)

HUTTON. Thank goodness! Janet, we're still friends, aren't we?
JANET (*rising and moving up* C) Of course we are. Better than
ever. And how we shall chuckle over this, when we come to look
back on it. The little joke you played on me, and the little joke
(*she turns*) I played on you.
HUTTON. The joke?
JANET. Why, of course. You didn't think I was serious, did
you?
HUTTON (*hesitating, then forcing a laugh*) No, no. Naturally, I
didn't.
JANET (*moving to the end of the sofa*) And when shall I have the
pleasure of meeting your sweet little . . . What's her name, by the
way? (*She sits on the* L *arm of the sofa with her back to Hutton*)
HUTTON. Doris.
JANET. Your sweet little Doris. When are you going to—to
inaugurate her?

(*There is a noise on the verandah up* C)

(*She rises*) What's that? (*She moves to the window up* C)
GENERAL (*off; calling*) Janet, are you there?

(JANET *opens the window.* HUTTON *rises, blows out the lamp, picks
it up, moves up* C *and places it on the cabinet*)

JANET. Father! Father, are you soaked?

(*The* NURSE, *pushing a wheelchair in which* GENERAL SPENCE *is
seated, enters up* C)

HUTTON. Good evening, General.
NURSE. Just a little bit wet, Miss Spence.
GENERAL. Good evening, Hutton. Nonsense, it's stopped rain-
ing—damned woman.
NURSE. Really, General! (*To Hutton*) Good evening.

(JANET *moves on to the verandah and looks off* R)

HUTTON. Good evening. Well, General, this is like campaign-
ing in the monsoon.
GENERAL. You're right, sir.

Hutton. Forgive this domestic disarray—I only got here an hour ago.

General. Sorry to load ourselves on you. Libbard picked us up while we were sheltering, and insisted on our coming here—pushed me half the way in this hearse.

Hutton. Why didn't he come in?

General. Went back for his car.

(Libbard *enters up* c *from* R. Janet *follows him in and shuts the windows*)

Fancy being a doctor. Good God, what a job!

Libbard (*easing down* RC) I couldn't agree more. I suggest you make the job a bit easier and get yourself rubbed down with a dry towel. Would you mind, Hutton?

Hutton. Of course not. (*To the Nurse*) You know where the towels are kept. Take whatever you need.

Nurse. Thank you, I will. (*She starts to wheel the General toward the door up* L)

General. Where the devil are you taking me?

(Hutton *opens the doors up* L, *then moves to the cabinet up* C, *opens it, takes out a decanter of whisky, a syphon of soda, and two glasses, and puts them on the top of the cabinet*)

Nurse (*in the tone of one who tries to calm a naughty child*) Now, now, now. No swearing.

(*The* Nurse *wheels the General off* L, *closing the doors behind her*)

Hutton (*to Libbard*) Have a drink?

Libbard. Thank you.

(Hutton *pours out two drinks*)

Janet (*moving down* R) Guess what Henry has brought back from Cornwall, Dr Libbard?

Libbard (*sitting on the upstage arm of the easy chair*) Well, what does one bring back from Cornwall? I seem to remember paper-weights made of malachite—no, serpentine; isn't that the stuff?

Janet. It isn't a paper-weight. It's alive.

(Hutton *moves to Libbard and gives him a drink, then sits with his own on the stool*)

Libbard. Alive? Well, one used to be able to get the most wonderful parrots at Falmouth. Brought back by the sailors. And what a vocabulary! Is it one of those?

Janet (*moving up* C; *shaking her head*) It's a mammal.

Hutton (*protesting*) Janet!

Janet. Well, isn't it?

Libbard. A mammal. Well, let's say a dog? A pony? A marmoset? A badger? I give it up. A Siamese cat?

(JANET *shakes her head after each suggestion and eases to the doors up* L)

JANET. A wife.

(JANET *turns and exits up* L)

LIBBARD. Well, I suppose I ought to congratulate you, Hutton.
HUTTON. Thank you.
LIBBARD. And yet, I posted that letter you gave me. Most faithfully. It wasn't quite as irrevocable as you thought?
HUTTON. No, it wasn't. (*He pauses*) Do you remember in the Gospels—all those people possessed by devils? Nobody believes in that sort of thing nowadays. And yet, isn't it the most plausible explanation of some of the things we do? Things that we know are against our own interest. Things that are obviously wrong and idiotic and suicidal. And yet, we do them. Or is it somebody else, inside, that does them in spite of us?
LIBBARD. Well, that's one way of disclaiming responsibility. The other way, the more modern way, is to call the devils traumas and complexes, and say it's all your mother's fault for having weaned you too early. And probably she *did* wean you too soon, and perhaps there *are* devils. But, there's also such a thing as free will.
HUTTON. Yes, there's such a thing as free will; and you can use your will to get rid of your will.
LIBBARD. That's the purpose of religion, isn't it? "Not I, but God in me."
HUTTON. And what about "not I but trauma in me. Not I but complex; not I but Lucifer. Not I but Belial in me—Belial, Eros, Priapus"?
LIBBARD (*rising*) Yes, if you don't have the right religion you've got to have one of the wrong ones, however bad and dangerous, provided it's a reasonably effective substitute for the genuine article. (*He puts his glass on the writing-table*)
HUTTON. And Belial's probably the most effective.
LIBBARD. Not for everybody. It's always difficult to understand other people's vices. Drink, for example. I just haven't the faintest idea why anybody should wish to narcotize himself with alcohol. And even sex. I've always been much more tempted by power and money. I've had to resist those pretty strenuously. But sensuality was never too difficult. (*He sits on the downstage arm of the easy chair*)
HUTTON. And yet there's nothing you can lose yourself in so completely. Nothing that so utterly abolishes your ordinary, every-day, free-will self.
LIBBARD. Nothing except the real thing.
HUTTON (*rising*) So they say. I've only tried the substitutes. (*He moves up* C *and puts his glass on the cabinet*)

LIBBARD. And that on your own showing is a possession by devils. And the devils make you do things that are idiotic and suicidal. In spite of which you go on.

HUTTON (*moving* R *of the sofa*) In spite of which and also because of which. After all, idiocy's a way of getting out of oneself. So's suicide. Not that I'd care to blow my brains out. But social suicide—there's something very fascinating about the idea of being ostracized, of being cut off from the group you've always belonged to, of losing one's collective personality and having to start afresh—a naked individual. (*He sits on the* R *arm of the sofa*) Alone in one's own resources. I tell you it has always fascinated me.

LIBBARD. And that's why you married?

HUTTON (*nodding*) To be ostracized. There were also other reasons, too.

LIBBARD. A child?

HUTTON. That's one of the reasons.

LIBBARD. That's the best news you've ever given me. We'll make a human being of you even yet.

HUTTON. Better not mention this to Janet. Not yet awhile.

LIBBARD. Of course not. (*He pauses*) She seems to have taken the news of your marriage in a very jocular spirit.

HUTTON. A bit too jocular. That's why I'd rather you said nothing about this other thing.

LIBBARD. She'll find out soon enough, of course.

HUTTON. Not as soon as all that. Doris and I are going abroad in a couple of days. I'd meant to do it without letting anyone know. But then this happened and—well, I felt I had to tell Janet about our marriage. Otherwise, I'd have kept it quiet for a few months. It would have made things easier. However . . . (*He shrugs his shoulders*) Everything, doubtless, is for the best in the best of all possible worlds.

(*The telephone rings*)

(*He moves to the telephone and lifts the receiver. Into the telephone*) Hullo . . . Oh, it's you . . .

(JANET *and the* NURSE *enter up* L)

JANET. Father's in need of a drink. Do you mind if I get him one?

HUTTON (*to Janet*) No, no, help yourself. You'll find glasses in the cupboard. (*Into the telephone*) No, no, stay where you are, I'll come and fetch you in the car. (*He replaces the receiver*)

(JANET *gets two glasses from the cabinet cupboard, and pours out two drinks*)

That was my wife. She went to see some friends. And now the roads are like rivers. (*He crosses to the writing-table*) Can I take you along, Libbard? (*He puts on his raincoat*)

LIBBARD (*rising*) No, thanks. I've got my car outside.

(JANET *hands a drink to the* NURSE, *who exits with it up* L)

HUTTON (*to Janet*) I'll be back in a few minutes; then I'll run you over to your house.

JANET. Thank you, Henry. And, meanwhile, I'll have a chance of meeting your sweet little Dora.

HUTTON (*moving to the window up* C) Doris.

JANET. Of course.

(HUTTON *exits up* C)

LIBBARD. I've taken too much time off already. (*He moves to the window up* C) I'll be looking in to see your father one day early next week.

JANET. All right.

(LIBBARD *exits up* C.

The NURSE, *carrying a rug, enters up* L. JANET, *carrying her drink, eases* R)

NURSE. Your father's tired. He's going to have a nap.

JANET. I'm glad. It's good for him to sleep.

NURSE (*moving to the fireplace*) It's not my place to say anything; but, if you ask me, I think it's disgusting. (*She switches on the electric radiator*) Getting married six weeks after that poor angel breathed her last. Six weeks! Shameful, that's what it is.

JANET. Don't take it too seriously.

NURSE (*holding out the rug to dry at the radiator*) And how does he have the face to stand there and talk about "my wife"—just like that. It gave me quite a turn. To think that there he is as if nothing had happened, with that woman round the corner somewhere. And that poor angel hardly cold in her grave. It makes me absolutely sick to think of it.

JANET. He told me he'd known her several months. That means that, even while Emily was alive . . .

NURSE. Didn't I tell you so? You wouldn't believe me; but you see.

JANET. I'm glad poor Emily never knew.

NURSE. I'm not. I wish she'd found him out. I'd have liked to hear her tell him what she thought of him. Pigs—that's what they are, every one of them.

JANET. I don't know how they dare. I'd be so nervous of being caught.

NURSE. *You* would, yes. But men have no shame, no decent feelings.

JANET. All the same, it must have come as a great relief to him.

NURSE. You mean, when she died?

JANET. Well, he wanted to marry her, didn't he?

NURSE. How do we know he didn't *have* to marry her?

Janet (*moving to the cabinet*) You mean, she was . . .? (*She puts her glass on the cabinet*)

Nurse (*nodding emphatically*) I'd be ready to bet on it. He gets her in trouble, and then he has to get her out again.

Janet (*moving down* c) And if Emily hadn't died just when she did—what then?

Nurse. Oh, there's plenty of shady doctors. Not quacks, mind you—real, good doctors. It costs a bit of money, of course. I could tell you a thing or two . . .

Janet. But, luckily for them she did die. Just at the right moment.

(*The* Nurse *looks at her for a moment in silence*)

Nurse. Just at the right moment. (*She pauses*) Miss Spence, you don't suppose . . .? (*She breaks off*)

Janet. Suppose what?

Nurse. Why wouldn't he let me take the medicine up to her? He'd never done that before.

Janet. He knew you were in a hurry. I thought it was very nice of him.

Nurse (*draping the rug over the chair down* l) Nice of him? He never did anything nice for me. I wouldn't have wanted him to, what's more. (*She moves* r *of the sofa*) No, Miss Spence, whatever he did, he did because it suited him. He took that medicine up to her, because he'd got some reason for it.

Janet (*sitting on the downstage arm of the easy chair*) You're not suggesting that—well, that he put something into it? That's too absurd.

Nurse (*moving up* c) Do you remember? Standing there in the verandah. It was printed on the label. "Poison. Contains Arsenic."

Janet. What *are* you talking about?

Nurse (*turning*) Arsenic, arsenic. Brings on vomiting. Something terrible—I've seen it. So *that* was why he made all that fuss about the red-currants. Just to give himself an alibi.

Janet. You're mad! It's absolutely ridiculous.

Nurse (*moving down* c) You thought it was ridiculous when I told you he was carrying on with a girl. Well, who was right— you or me?

Janet. But, that's different.

Nurse. It starts differently. But, look where it ends. Lies and tricks and quarrels. And before you know where you are, some-body's asking for a divorce—or else somebody dies. (*She moves* l) Dies in the nick of time. Dies, just because a man suddenly can't do without sex. (*She adjusts the rug, turning the other side to the radiator*)

Janet. But, I've known him for years. He couldn't have done anything like that.

Nurse. You've known *a* Mr Hutton. The one that talks so

nicely about art and all that sort of thing. But you've never known the one that can't keep his hands off girls, the one that'll do anything for the sake of sex. Anything, I tell you, anything. The more I think of it, the worse it looks. Why did it happen on the day I was out?

JANET. What difference did that make?

NURSE (*moving* C) What difference? Why, if I'd been there he could never have got away with it. I've seen arsenic cases. I'd have recognized the symptoms immediately. So what does he do? Chooses the day when he knows I won't be back till late—till it's all over, in fact. Then he goes out himself—on the tiles, most likely, with that girl of his. (*She sits on the sofa*)

JANET. He wouldn't have done that!

NURSE. Oh yes he would. You don't know what they're like. And when he gets home he turns on me and says I killed her with those red-currants. Currants, indeed.

JANET. But, after all, Dr Libbard thought it was the currants.

NURSE. Yes—and why? Because the other one keeps harping on it. And so I have to take the blame, I'm the scapegoat, I'm the one to be crucified. But, I tell you, I'm not going to put up with it any longer. And it's not merely a question of my own interests. It's a matter of principle. I want to see justice done. I want to have the whole world know the truth.

JANET. You talk as though you knew it yourself.

NURSE (*rising*) Well, I do. (*She moves to the fireplace*)

JANET. You don't. You're getting over-excited and imagining things.

NURSE (*turning*) I tell you, Miss Spence, I'm as certain about it now as I would be if they'd already had the autopsy.

JANET. The autopsy?

NURSE. Yes, the autopsy.

JANET. Do you mean to talk to Dr Libbard?

NURSE. Dr Libbard? No, of course not. He wouldn't want to admit he'd made a mistake. He'd try to talk me out of it. Besides, all he could do would be to report to the authorities. (*She leans over the back of the sofa*) No, I've got my contacts, I know who to go to.

JANET. And suppose they did find something in the body?

NURSE. They'll ask who put it there. And when they ask that, they'll find only one possible answer.

JANET (*rising*) Only one answer?

(*Voices are heard off up* C)

NURSE. Yes, and here it is. In person.

(DORIS, *followed by* HUTTON, *enters up* C)

HUTTON. If we have much more of this, I shall start building an ark. (*He leads* DORIS *to* JANET) Well, my dear, this is Doris. As a matter of fact, you've seen her before. Do you remember?

JANET. The crippled children! (*She laughs*) That *was* a good joke wasn't it?

DORIS (*overcome by shyness and embarrassment*) Oh—er—yes.

HUTTON. This is Nurse Braddock. General Spence's nurse.

NURSE (*severely*) How do you do—*Mrs Hutton*. I used to look after Mr Hutton's wife before she died.

HUTTON (*moving to the doors up* L) That's scarcely the expression I should have chosen. I'll get the cases down.

(HUTTON *exits up* L, *leaving the door open*)

JANET. Do you mind if I call you "Doris"? You know, it seems ridiculous for me to be calling you "Mrs Hutton".

DORIS. I'd love it.

JANET. And you must call me Janet.

DORIS. Yes, Miss Spence—I mean, Janet.

JANET. Isn't she adorable! My dear, what a lovely brooch! Don't I recognize it?

DORIS. Yes, it belonged to—to Mrs Hutton. I mean—you know. (*She sits on the sofa*)

JANET. Of course. Emily's diamond dragonfly. (*To the Nurse*) Do you see, Nurse?

NURSE (*bitterly*) I'd noticed it already. (*She switches off the radiator*)

JANET. I remember how much you admired it. (*She moves to* Doris) Nurse Braddock used to be a great friend of poor Emily's before—before she came to help me with my father. She was really more of a friend than a nurse.

NURSE. It isn't friendship that gets you diamond brooches. (*She folds the rug*)

JANET. But, it gets you diamond bracelets all right. (*She shows* Doris *her bracelet*) See what your husband has just given me.

NURSE. He gave you that?

JANET. This afternoon. Wasn't that sweet of him? (*To Doris*) Aren't you a little jealous?

DORIS. Of course not.

JANET. "Of course not." You're a real flatterer, aren't you? (*She holds the bracelet close to Doris's neck*) This is how the stones ought to be shown off—against really young skin. Skin that's smooth and tight. Tell me, Doris, are you very, very happy?

DORIS. Yes, I—I think so.

JANET. You only think so?

DORIS (*painfully embarrassed*) No, no, I don't mean *that*.

GENERAL (*off; calling*) Nurse, Nurse, where are you?

NURSE (*moving to the doors up* L) Excuse me, Miss Spence.

(*The* NURSE *exits with the rug up* L)

JANET. I'm sorry. Let's talk about something else, if it upsets you.

DORIS. But I *am* happy. Really and truly. It's just—you know, I'm not very clever. And Henry seems to know everything. I'd like to have some lessons, or something—you know, about art and things.

JANET (*sitting on the stool*) You sweet child!

DORIS. Then I'd know the difference between things. I mean, some pictures *look* funny; but they aren't meant to *be* funny. You have to know which is which, don't you?

JANET. Well, yes, it's advisable.

(*The* NURSE, *followed by* HUTTON, *wheels the* GENERAL *in up* L, *places the chair up* C *facing front, then stands above it*)

GENERAL. What's all this about Hutton getting married again? Hullo, Hutton. You're a more sensible fellow than I thought.

(JANET *rises and moves to the window* R)

HUTTON. Thank you, General.

GENERAL. This is the "happy bride", I presume.

HUTTON (*introducing them*) This is Doris. Doris—General Spence.

DORIS. How do you do?

(HUTTON *exits up* L)

GENERAL (*to Doris*) Take that ridiculous hat off.

(DORIS *removes her hat*)

That's better. (*To Janet*) She's the image of your mother, when we were engaged. Same hair, same eyes. But I'd say the nose was a tiny bit more retroussé. (*To Doris*) Turn your head.

(DORIS *obediently turns her head a little*)

(*To Janet*) Do you remember, Janet, that photograph of her in the riding habit? That's the thing she was wearing when I saw her first. Dark green, and she was riding a grey gelding. (*To Doris*) Don't you ever ride in anything but a habit, my dear. No breeches. Women aren't the right shape for breeches. Whereas, in a riding habit—well, a man could still have illusions. And what's life without illusions?

(HUTTON, *carrying a suitcase, enters up* L. *He places the suitcase* R *of the cabinet up* C, *then moves* L *of the sofa*)

Nasty, solitary, brutish and short. And women's legs are shorter than life. (*To Hutton*) Do you hear that, Hutton? No breeches. If my wife had worn breeches I'd never have married her.

HUTTON (*perching himself on the back of the sofa*) And Janet would have remained a twinkle in your eye.

GENERAL (*noisily*) It's about time she became a twinkle in somebody else's eye. Don't you agree, Hutton?

NURSE. Now, now, don't get so excited.

GENERAL. I will get excited if I choose. It's about time she thought of herself for a change. Time she stopped this damned self-sacrifice. I'm not worth it. I ought to have been dead ten years ago. Tell her to let me go to blazes and find herself a husband.

JANET. Have you anyone in mind, Father? Or you, Henry? Have you any suggestions?

GENERAL. That's up to you, my girl. When a girl sets her cap at a man, she usually gets what she wants in the long run. It's up to you. We don't want you to end your days as one of those damned spinsters. (*To Doris*) This little filly knew what she was about. You're a wise and lucky young woman.

DORIS. Yes, I'm lucky.

NURSE (*moving to the windows up* C) Are you?

HUTTON. What exactly do you mean by that, Nurse Braddock?

NURSE. I'm going to get in touch with the authorities. I have something to say of interest to the coroner.

(*The* NURSE *turns and exits up* C)

CURTAIN

SCENE 2

SCENE—*The same. Afternoon. July.*

The decorators have departed, the dust sheets have been removed and the room is again habitable. There has been some further re-arrangement of the furniture. The sofa is back in its Act I position LC *with the occasional tables* R *and* L *of it. The telephone and lamp are on the table* L *of the sofa. The library steps are against the bookshelves above the fireplace, and the easy chair is down* L, *with the stool* R *of it. The writing-table stands between the windows. The armchair is down* C *facing* L. *The easel has been removed, and a pedestal with a small statue on it now stands in the alcove down* R.

(*See the Ground Plan at the end of the Play*)

When the CURTAIN *rises, the doors up* L *are closed; the windows are closed, and the curtains open.* DORIS, *wearing a négligé, is lying on the sofa, facing* R *and covered by an eiderdown. A child's teddy-bear on the sofa, and a golliwog on the floor down* L *reflect her tastes. She is speaking into the telephone.*

DORIS (*into the telephone*) No, I wasn't there. Henry didn't want me to go. Besides, I've still got a bit of a cold . . . He isn't back yet. I don't think it'll be over for another hour or so . . . But, Auntie, there isn't any doubt about it . . . Of course, it'll be all right . . . Why an inquest? Just out of spite—nothing else.

B*

They're angry because we didn't wait a year . . . And then they're all a hundred years old, so they simply hate me . . . No, she's all right, she's been awfully nice really. And her father likes me, too. He's sweet.

(JANET *enters quietly up* L)

(*She beckons to Janet to come in. Into the telephone*) Listen, I've got to ring off now. Janet has just come in for tea. I'll call you up again later . . . Good-bye. (*She stretches over the back of the sofa and replaces the receiver*)

JANET (*moving* R *of the sofa; gushingly*) Well, well. Sitting there with all her toys around her like a dear little girl. (*She picks up the teddy-bear*) Too sweet.

DORIS. Janet, you don't look well. What's the matter?

JANET (*moving to the armchair down* C) I'm perfectly all right. (*She sits and nurses the teddy-bear*)

DORIS. Are you still sleeping so badly?

JANET. Oh, that's nothing. And, anyhow, Libbard's promised to give me some kind of a pill. From now on I shall snore.

DORIS. You've been worrying too much, Janet.

JANET. Is that surprising? After all, Henry's a very old friend.

DORIS. *I* don't worry. I *know* everything's going to be all right.

JANET (*after a pause*) Have you heard what happened at the inquest?

DORIS. No. Have you?

JANET. Nothing, except that today they were only going to hear the medical evidence.

DORIS (*shuddering*) It's horrible. Digging up somebody after they're dead. And for no reason. Just because there's some spiteful gossip. That beastly nurse of yours! I can't understand why you keep her.

JANET. Now, dear, don't be unreasonable. You know quite well I wanted to send her away; but Henry wouldn't hear of it; nor would Doctor Libbard. Sending her away would have meant that we took her seriously. And that's the last impression we want to give.

DORIS. She ought to be punished—that's what I feel.

JANET. We can think of that later on, when—when all this is over.

DORIS. Henry and I are going abroad again, next week.

(CLARA, *carrying the tray of tea, enters up* L, *moves down* L, *puts the tray on the stool, turns and exits up* L)

JANET. Oh, you're going abroad again?

DORIS. We were having such a wonderful time in Italy. And then to be called back for this nonsense. And the workmen still in the house.

JANET (*rising and putting the teddy-bear and her handbag down on her chair*) That's the last straw. (*She moves to the easy chair and sits*)

DORIS (*looking at her watch*) Henry ought to be back pretty soon.

JANET (*pouring out the tea*) How was he, when he went off this morning? A bit worried, I suppose.

DORIS. No. He was too angry to be worried. It makes him so furious, the way they're treating him.

JANET (*ironically*) As though he were a member of the un-privileged classes. (*She suddenly changes her tone to one of solicitude*) Darling, how dreadfully unkind of me. I quite forgot to ask how you've been. Is everything going as it ought to go? (*She rises and hands Doris a cup of tea*)

DORIS. Well, I still feel sick in the morning, if that's what you mean.

JANET (*easing to the fireplace*) And Libbard's pleased with you, is he?

DORIS. He seems to be.

JANET (*after a pause; reflectively*) It must be a very strange and wonderful thing.

DORIS. You mean, to be going to have a baby?

(JANET *nods*)

Oh, I suppose it'll be all right when the baby's actually there. But now—I think I'd rather have the measles again. At least it doesn't last so long.

JANET (*after a pause*) Are you going to nurse your baby your-self?

DORIS. I don't know. I hadn't thought about it.

JANET. I would, if I had one. I wouldn't feel it was really mine, if I didn't.

(CLARA *enters up* L)

CLARA. Nurse Braddock would like to speak to you, madam.

DORIS. Ask her to come in.

(CLARA *exits up* L)

JANET (*sitting in the easy chair down* L) What can she want?

(*The* NURSE *enters up* L)

NURSE (*moving* C) Good afternoon, Mrs Hutton. I hope you won't mind my bursting in like this. Oh, Miss Spence, as it's my afternoon off I told your father you would be back with him for tea.

JANET. Yes, I see.

DORIS. Would you like a cup of tea?

NURSE. No, thank you. Mrs Hutton, I realize quite well what you must be thinking of me. Officious and silly, that's what you think I am. I know. But in view of what's happened I feel I was fully justified in doing my duty.

JANET. What do you mean? In view of what's happened?

NURSE. I feel I ought to warn you, Mrs Hutton. You're young and impressionable. I suppose we all make mistakes from time to time.

JANET. What are you talking about? (*She drinks her tea*)

NURSE. I've just left Dr Libbard. He'd come straight from the inquest. The man from the Home Office gave his evidence. They found arsenic in the body.

DORIS. But that's a poison!

NURSE. It's got hardly any taste. That's why so many murderers use it.

JANET. That's enough.

NURSE. But you said . . .

JANET. I think you'd better go.

NURSE. Why does everyone turn on me? I was only trying to help. I thought I ought to warn this poor child of the danger she was running. I . . .

DORIS. Please go.

NURSE (*taking a bottle of tablets from her handbag; to Janet*) Doctor Libbard asked me to give you this. (*She puts the bottle on the table* R *of the sofa. To Doris*) Well, don't say I didn't warn you.

(*The* NURSE *turns and exits up* L)

DORIS (*without looking at Janet*) What will they do now, Janet?

JANET. Well, the coroner's jury will have to decide how the poison came to be where it was. And then, if somebody's suspected, there'd have to be a trial.

DORIS. Janet, do you think . . .? I mean, could they do something to him?

JANET. To Henry? But Henry hasn't done anything.

DORIS. No, but suppose he had? (*She puts her cup on the table* L *of the sofa*)

JANET. Doris, you mustn't say those things.

DORIS. But just suppose . . . Then they *could* do something, couldn't they?

JANET. Well, you know what happens to people who—who kill someone.

DORIS. Oh, it's too awful. (*She covers her face with her hands and starts to cry*)

(JANET *looks at her intently for a moment, then rises and moves* R *of the sofa*)

JANET. Darling, don't cry. It'll be all right.

DORIS. Don't, please.

(JANET *takes a tablet from the bottle on the table* R *of the sofa and offers it to Doris*)

JANET. Take this, dear.

DORIS (*taking a handkerchief from her handbag*) I don't want anything. (*She dabs her eyes*)

JANET. It's what Dr Libbard's given me for sleeping. One tablet. Just enough to calm your nerves a little, that's all.

DORIS. Leave me alone. Please.

JANET. Do it for Henry's sake. Think how upset he'll be if he comes home and finds you in this state.

(DORIS *uncovers her face and wipes her eyes*)

DORIS (*picking up her teacup*) Thank you, Janet. (*She takes the tablet, swallows it, then takes a gulp of tea*) Thank you, Janet. You've been an angel. (*She puts her handkerchief away and the cup on the table* L *of the sofa*)

JANET. You'll feel quieter in a moment, dear.

DORIS. Janet, isn't there anything he could do?

JANET. Well, he's doing it. He's answering their questions; he's explaining why it couldn't be him.

DORIS. But if he can't explain . . . Couldn't he go away somewhere and hide?

JANET. I suppose he could, if he went far enough. (*She gets her handbag from the chair down* C) I must get back to my father. He gets so impatient if I'm late for his game of chess. (*She kisses Doris*) Good-bye, darling, and don't fret. You'll see—tomorrow it'll all be explained, and then you'll live happily ever after.

(JANET *exits up* L.

DORIS *sits in silence for a moment, then rises, moves above the table* L *of the sofa, refers to the telephone index, and lifts the telephone receiver*)

DORIS (*into the telephone*) I want to put a call through to London . . . Eight-four-double-o Mayfair . . . (*She perches herself on the back of the sofa*) Hullo, Overseas Airways? . . . Good afternoon . . . I want to ask about booking seats on a plane . . . Yes, I'll hold on . . . Hullo. I want to ask about tickets. If I wanted to book two seats on a plane, could I do it at the last moment? . . . Where to? Oh, Italy . . . Yes, Rome, that's right. And you think there might be a chance of getting seats even if I made up my mind by tonight? . . . What time does it leave? . . . (*She rises*)

(HUTTON *enters up* L. *He moves to the sofa and sits down heavily at the* R *end of it, with a sigh of utter weariness, and closes his eyes*)

Thank you. I'm much obliged. (*She replaces the receiver. To Hutton*) Darling, are you feeling all right?

(HUTTON *nods*)

(*She moves below the sofa*) I've just heard what happened. It's too terrible—isn't it?

HUTTON. It's terrible, because it's impossible and yet it's happened.

DORIS. But how . . .?

HUTTON. Don't ask any questions, darling. Don't let's talk about it. Not now. (*He puts his hand on his head*) It's all a confusion. Like a dust storm. No, worse than that. Like being in the middle of a swarm of insects. I just can't think about it any more. (*He reaches out a hand to draw her toward him*)

DORIS (*shrinking away*) Henry, no . . .

(HUTTON *ignores her protest and, putting an arm about her, draws her down on to the sofa and for a long time she lies in the crook of his arm. He kisses her*)

HUTTON. This is impossible, too—impossibly good, for a change—and yet it happens. It's happening now. How does a piece of matter set about falling in love or writing *Hamlet*? It's just out of the question. And yet, there *Hamlet* is; and there are you, and here am I. Defying time, outside this nightmare of perpetual perishing, beyond evil, beyond good.

"There is no future, there is no more past,
    No roots nor fruits, but momentary flowers;
    Lie still, only lie still, and night will last,
    Dark and silent, not for a space of hours,
    But everlastingly . . ."

DORIS (*after a long silence*) Darling, I never knew you loved me as much as that.

HUTTON (*with a tenderly mocking smile*) As much as what? As much as this? (*He kisses her on her forehead and mouth*) Or as this? (*He kisses the back of her neck*) Or as this?

DORIS. Oh, *why* did you do it, Henry? Why *did* you do it?

(*The question arouses* HUTTON's *anger. He pushes her away from him and rises*)

HUTTON. Why did I do it? (*He crosses to the fireplace*) You all seem to take it for granted that I murdered my wife. First, there's the coroner. Did I put anything into Emily's medicine? Then old Johnson cuts me dead in the street outside the court. (*He strides* C *and turns*) And now you. You! (*All his pent-up exasperation, fear and bewilderment are turned into a violent and senseless fury against Doris. He picks up the teddy-bear from the chair down* C) Wring its neck and get a new one. (*He tears the teddy-bear's head from its body and throws the dismembered fragments on the floor*) I suppose you imagined I was so insanely in love that I'd do anything to get you—anything, anything. It's about time women realized that men don't go insane about them. All one asks for is a little amusement and a chance to forget oneself . . . (*He breaks off and shrugs his shoulders in a gesture of frustration*)

DORIS (*rising*) Please, Henry, don't, don't.

HUTTON. I don't know why the devil I ever married you. Why any man in his right mind ever married any woman, for that matter. I've had enough.

DORIS (*imploringly*) Henry. Henry.

HUTTON *turns, strides to the window up* C *and exits.*

DORIS *hurries to the window after him, pauses, turns, moves down* C, *picks up the teddy-bear, attempts to replace its head, then drops it on the armchair down* C, *moves to the table* R *of the sofa, picks up the bottle of sleeping tablets and drops sobbing to her knees below the sofa. As she pours the tablets into her hand—*

the CURTAIN *falls*

When the CURTAIN *rises after a few moments, it is some hours later and dusk has fallen. The lamp on the table* L *of the sofa is lit.* DORIS, *covered by the eiderdown, is lying on the sofa.* LIBBARD *is standing by the writing-table, closing his bag.*

LIBBARD. Well, that's that, young woman. A day in bed and you can do what you like. And remember, no more of this sort of nonsense.

DORIS (*with feeble defiance*) What's to prevent me?

LIBBARD. Nothing—except your own common sense and common decency. (*He turns and moves below the* R *end of the sofa*)

DORIS. He doesn't love me. I don't want to go on living.

LIBBARD. Who cares about what you want? Why not think of somebody else, for a change?

DORIS (*indignantly*) I think of Henry all the time.

LIBBARD. No, you don't. You think of yourself in relation to Henry. If you thought of Henry, you'd be trying to do something kind and useful—trying to help a man who's in a horribly tight corner. Instead of that, you make a nuisance of yourself by swallowing half a bottle of sleeping tablets. And, remember, if you wake up in the night with cramps in your intestine, don't blame Henry. It's entirely your own fault. Meanwhile, keep this on your tummy. (*He picks up the hot-water bottle from the table* R *of the sofa, and tucks it under the eiderdown*) There. (*He readjusts the eiderdown*) Now, what have you got to say for yourself?

DORIS. I'm sorry, Dr Libbard. I won't do it again.

(LIBBARD *smiles with genuine warmth and tenderness, and pats her hand*)

LIBBARD. Good girl. (*He moves to the writing-table and picks up his bag*)

DORIS. No, I'm not good. I've done dreadful things. That's why all this is happening. You heard what they said at the inquest, did you? Do you think—I mean, is it possible . . .

LIBBARD (*moving* c) No, I feel sure it wasn't Henry—if that's what you mean. (*He puts his case on the armchair down* c)

DORIS. Oh, I'm so thankful. But, then who—how did it happen?

LIBBARD. It might very easily have been suicide.

DORIS. Do you really think so?

LIBBARD (*smiling*) Well, you tried it, didn't you? I'm very fond of Henry; but I confess I'm glad I'm not married to him. (*He sits on the* R *arm of the sofa*)

DORIS. That isn't fair, Dr Libbard. It was my fault, not Henry's. After all, why *should* he love me, if he doesn't want to? It's my business to love him. Tell me how I can help him, Dr Libbard.

LIBBARD. Well, first of all, you've got to believe in him— through thick and thin and in spite of everything. That's the first thing. And then, whatever happens, you've got to be strong and calm. No tears, no harrowing scenes. They're just an indulgence, that's all. Some women cry as easily as pigs grunt, and they enjoy it very nearly as much. So don't do it. Don't do it. And finally remember you're going to have a baby. That'll probably be about the best thing that ever happened to Henry. So, for goodness' sake don't let's make a mess of it.

(HUTTON *enters quietly up* L)

HUTTON (*moving above the sofa*) Is it all right if I come in now, Libbard? I've been waiting upstairs for three hours. Is she all right?

LIBBARD. Flourishing.

HUTTON. Hullo, darling.

DORIS. Hullo.

(LIBBARD *rises and picks up his bag*)

LIBBARD. How wonderful it would be if we were all dis-embodied spirits. Then there wouldn't have to be any doctors— only psychoanalysts at five guineas an hour.

HUTTON. I'm so thankful you got here in time.

LIBBARD (*moving to the doors up* L) Good night, Henry; and if it's any comfort to you, I *don't* draw the obvious conclusions from the medical evidence.

HUTTON. Thank you.

(LIBBARD *exits up* L)

(*He moves* c) I'm sorry, darling.

DORIS. I'm the one who's sorry. I was just trying to spite you, trying to get my own back.

HUTTON. I began it, I'm afraid. (*He sits beside her on the edge of the sofa*)

DORIS. But *I* ought to have known better.

HUTTON (*smiling*) At twenty-two?

DORIS. This is something where it doesn't make any difference how old you are. It's just a question of—well, of being a *girl*. No, I hate that word; it's all wrong. Why can't women call themselves women? Why do they have to pretend they're like those faces in the movies? You know—always looking at men out of the corners of their eyes. I do it myself, of course. Why?—I don't know. But, of course, it isn't any different. I love you just as much in *that* way. Only, now, there's something else. Do you know what I mean?

HUTTON. Yes, I know what you mean.

DORIS. And to think I tried to kill myself. And everything's so beautiful. So—mysterious. (*She looks around the room*) Even that fly on the ceiling. Even that silly old doll. (*She moves her hand back and forth*) And this—how wonderful this is. Simply being able to move from one place to another. It's empty here, it's empty there. That's why you're free. Perhaps that's what God is—the emptiness between things. Free! Free! (*She moves her hand to various positions in space*) And then not free. (*She touches her own breast*) Not free. Just think if there were no emptiness, if everything were jam full, so that you couldn't move, like—like a coffin. That's death, that's hell. (*She pauses*) Darling, let's call him Patrick.

HUTTON. Call whom?

DORIS. I mean—if it's a boy.

HUTTON. Oh, I see. Well, I'm not an Irishman; but I don't have any objection to Patrick. And if it's a girl?

DORIS. Well, what about Belinda?

HUTTON. No, there I draw the line.

DORIS. But it's such a pretty name.

HUTTON. Do you see me running after the child in Kensington Gardens and yelling, "Belinda, Belinda"?

DORIS. You'd look silly whatever her name was. Any man looks silly, when he's trying to keep a tiny child in order.

HUTTON. But I'd rather not look sillier than necessary.

DORIS. All right, then; we'll call her something else. Oh, it's going to be so wonderful. They'll go to school and they'll grow up, and they'll marry, and then there'll be grandchildren.

HUTTON. And, meanwhile, there'll have been two or three more world wars and half a dozen slumps and revolutions. But, fortunately, private life will still go on, as it always has done, in spite of everything the benefactors of humanity can do to us. The great men are acclaimed and then hated; the empires rise and fall; the religions flourish and decay; the ideologies come into fashion and go out again. But the business of eating and drinking and talking and loving—it's still the only thing that really matters. It isn't progress or evolution that can make people happy; it's sitting on the grass and looking at the sunset and, maybe, surreptitiously picking one's nose.

DORIS. They shall not pick their noses.

HUTTON. That's what *you* say. But, just wait and see. Even Belinda will do it. Even Isolde. Even Melisande.

DORIS (*putting her hand over his mouth*) Stop it. (*Suddenly her expression changes*) Henry, we've forgotten. We're just shutting our eyes and pretending. Listen. Just before you came back from the court I rang up Overseas Airways. They say that, with luck, you can get seats at the last moment. I'm well enough. I could get up now if I had to.

HUTTON. Who put this idiotic idea into your head?

DORIS. Oh, you don't think it's a good plan?

HUTTON (*sarcastically*) Excellent, if you want to get me tried for murder. Can't you see—it would be simply asking them to arrest me?

DORIS. I hadn't thought of that.

HUTTON. Of course not—because you still believe I did it.

DORIS. But I don't, I don't.

HUTTON. Then why do you suggest that I should run away?

DORIS. Well, I thought it would be safer. I mean, just in case they didn't understand. In case you couldn't make them believe. Oh, I've been a fool again. I've made you angry. It's only because I love you so much—because I was so terribly anxious . . .

HUTTON. I said something very stupid this afternoon. I said I didn't know why I'd married you. Well, perhaps I didn't know then, but I do now. I know very well.

DORIS. Why?

HUTTON. Because—I love my love with an L, because she is so logical. So lamentable at the same time and so lachrymose. Not to mention so little, so light, so lithe, so lovely. And so ludicrous. (*He taps her on the nose*)

(*There is a knock at the door up* L)

(*He calls*) Come in.

(CLARA *enters up* L)

CLARA. It's Miss Spence, sir. She says she doesn't want to disturb you; but she forgot something when she was here this afternoon.

HUTTON (*to Doris*) Is it all right?

(DORIS *nods*)

(*To Clara*) Ask her to come in. (*He rises and moves to the fireplace*)

(CLARA *exits up* L)

What did she forget?

(DORIS *points to the bottle of sleeping tablets on the table* R *of the sofa*)

Oh, that. Well, in a certain sense I'm glad she left it. Aren't you?

(JANET *enters up* L)

HUTTON. Hullo, Janet.

JANET (*moving* C) Darling, I've just heard from Clara . . . Oh, it's too awful.

DORIS. I'm quite all right, Janet. Really.

JANET. Is that true, Henry?

HUTTON. Libbard got here almost immediately. There's no harm done.

JANET. Thank God! You know, I feel so guilty. (*She indicates the bottle of tablets*) If I'd been less absent-minded . . .

HUTTON. We're grateful to you that you weren't.

JANET. Grateful?

HUTTON. Of course, it was a pretty dangerous operation. But, it's turned out to be entirely successful. Hasn't it, darling?

(DORIS *nods and smiles at him tenderly*)

JANET (*forcing a little laugh*) Oh! Well, I'd better take my property and go. Two's company, three's none. (*She picks up the tablets and moves above the sofa*) Good-bye, darling. I know you'll be glad to get rid of me.

DORIS. No, I won't, Janet.

JANET. You little fibber. I think I ought to tell you, Henry. I met the vicar just now and then Colonel Brabazon joined us. They said the most terrible things.

HUTTON. About me?

JANET (*nodding*) Really dreadful.

HUTTON. Well, I suppose it's only to be expected.

JANET. I told them they had no right even to think that way, much less to talk. After all, it could have been an accident, it could have been suicide.

HUTTON. Well, it certainly wasn't what they think. So, there it is. Either accident or suicide. (*He pauses*) Poor Emily—she was always saying she was tired of life. I used to think it was just a figure of speech. I suppose I didn't *want* to know how unhappy she was. (*He lowers his voice*) I keep wondering if she hadn't heard something about . . .

JANET. Yes, it's quite possible.

HUTTON. Perhaps that was what drove her to it. God, what one can do to people!

JANET (*after a pause; slowly*) Yess, what one can do to people! Well . . .

(JANET *exits up* L)

CURTAIN

ACT III

SCENE—*The stage is divided, unequally, between a prison cell* R *and the living-room in the Spences' cottage* L. *October.*

Each set should have an independent gauze curtain so that when one set is illuminated, the other is in darkness, invisible and non-existent. The cell, which is on a rostrum two feet high, is stone-floored and white-walled. The door with a grille in its upper half is up C. *There is a small barred window high up in the wall* L. *The furniture consists of a pallet bed against the wall* R, *and a small table with two chairs, one above and one below it, against the wall* L.

The Spences' living-room is a nondescript room in a nineteenth-century house of indeterminate style. There is a deep-set casement window up C *with leaded panes and a built-in window-seat looking out over the garden. The fireplace is* R. *Between the fireplace and the back wall there is a shallow alcove with three or four built-in shelves. An arch up* L *leads to the front door and other parts of the cottage. The furniture is old and comfortable but rather shabby. There is an up-holstered armchair down* R *and another above the fireplace. A writing-table with a telephone on it and a chair to it stands down* L, *a cabinet* L *of the window up* C, *and a low table down* RC. *A club fender surrounds the fireplace. General Spence's travels have left their mark on the room in the form of Indian hangings and panoplies of oriental weapons. A gilded wooden Buddha and a dancing Krishna in bronze stand on the top shelf of the alcove up* R, *and a statuette of Kali on the mantelpiece. The other shelves of the alcove and the cabinet are filled with books, papers, ornaments, etc. The room is illuminated at night by a table-lamp on the downstage end of the mantelpiece. Prominently visible on the back wall,* R *of the window, is a large clock. The window is prettily curtained and the window-seat is fitted with cushions. The floor is carpeted.*

(See the Ground Plan at the end of the Play)

When the CURTAIN rises, it is an autumn afternoon. The R gauze is closed, the L gauze is open. Both sets are dimly lit. HUTTON is seated on the bed in the cell staring at the floor. As he lifts his head to the window, the LIGHTS in the cell go out and those in the Spences' living-room come up. The fire is burning cheerfully and JANET, looking ill and haggard, is seated on the window-seat up C facing L. The clock strikes four. She rises, moves to the armchair down R and sits fingering her bracelet. After a moment, the NURSE enters up L, pushing the GENERAL in his wheelchair. They are both warmly dressed for outdoors. The GENERAL, who has a rug around his knees, is holding a paper bag.

NURSE (*moving to the shelves up* R) Well, here we are, dear. All ready for our afternoon walk. (*She takes a tin of dog biscuits from the shelf and opens it*) You're sure you won't change your mind and come with us? (*She takes the tin to the General*)

JANET (*in a strange flat monotone*) No.

GENERAL. Going to start by feeding the dogs. (*He proceeds to fill the paper bag with biscuits from the tin*) Does you good to be with dogs for a change. Takes your mind off your troubles. Wouldn't have minded being a dog myself. Comfortable kennel. Free meals. Unlimited access to the females of the species.

(*The* NURSE *takes the tin up* R, *puts the lid on and replaces it on the shelf*)

And when you're old, they shoot you. No wheelchairs, no torture, no damned nurses. Just a bang and it's all over.

(*The* NURSE *takes a bottle of medicine and a glass from the shelf and pours out a dose*)

Put on your things and come with us.

JANET (*dully*) No, Father, I'd rather not.

NURSE (*moving with the glass to the General*) It would help you to sleep, if you took some exercise. (*She hands the General his medicine*)

JANET. Please!

NURSE. A good brisk walk—that's what you need, dear. And then five minutes of deep breathing. I'm a great believer in deep breathing.

(*The* GENERAL *drinks his medicine*)

That and abdominal massage. Up the ascending colon, then across, then down. (*She takes the empty glass from the General*) Up, across and then down. Forty or fifty times. I used to do it for Mrs Hutton. Every single day. (*She sighs and shakes her head*) Poor thing, poor thing. (*She replaces the empty glass and medicine bottle on the shelf*) Well, she'll sleep easier in her grave after next Friday. (*To the General*) Got your bag of biscuits? (*She turns the General's chair towards the arch up* L) Vengeance is mine, saith the Lord— and that's the truth, as he'll find out when they put the noose round his neck and spring the trap. (*She starts to push the wheelchair off up* L) Well, we'll be back for tea.

(*The front door bell rings.*
The NURSE *exits with the* GENERAL *up* L.
The MAID *enters up* L)

MAID. Dr Libbard, miss.

JANET (*rising and moving above the table* RC) All right.

(*The* MAID *exits.*
LIBBARD *and the* GENERAL *can be heard exchanging greetings off, then* LIBBARD *enters up* L)

LIBBARD (*moving* C) I was driving past the house. Thought I'd just drop in to see how things were going.

JANET. Father seems quite well. He's just gone out for his walk.

LIBBARD. And you? (*He looks at her closely*) Hm. Not much of a credit to your physician, I'm afraid.

JANET (*after a pause*) If I don't sleep tonight I shall go mad. (*She breaks to the fireplace*)

LIBBARD. You've still got some of that stuff I gave you, haven't you?

JANET (*turning*) It doesn't seem to work any more. I get the most awful dreams and wake up again. Couldn't you give me something that would simply *make* me sleep?

LIBBARD. I *could*. But I'd much rather not.

JANET (*her flat voice breaking*) You don't know what it's like, Dr Libbard. Night after night. I can't stand it any longer.

LIBBARD (*taking off his coat*) Any fool can stop the symptoms of insomnia. The difficulty is to find the cause—to find it, and then to remove it. (*He puts his coat over the chair down* L)

(*There is a pause*)

JANET (*sitting on the fender*) Well, it's going to be removed—next Friday.

LIBBARD. Next Friday? Oh, I see. (*He moves above the table* RC) Do you hate him as much as all that?

JANET. After all, it was proved, wasn't it? They proved that he killed Emily. How do you expect me not to hate him?

LIBBARD. Yet you used to be such good friends.

JANET. Never. I always felt there was something wrong somewhere.

LIBBARD (*sitting in the armchair above the fireplace*) And yet Emily thought that, if she died, you and he ought to get married.

JANET (*rising*) Married? But, that's monstrous. How dare you?

LIBBARD. I'm only repeating what she said. More than once as I remember.

JANET (*breaking down* R *with mounting fury*) Talking about me as though I were one of those women of his, as though I were the kind of slut that will tumble into bed with any man that comes along. It's disgusting. It's—it's obscene.

LIBBARD. I don't know what's so obscene about marriage.

JANET (*moving in to Libbard*) I won't have it.

LIBBARD (*suddenly professional*) Getting excited doesn't help you to sleep, does it? (*He feels her pulse*)

(JANET *recovers her self-control and answers in a normal voice*)

JANET. I'm sorry, Dr Libbard. (*She turns to the fireplace*)

LIBBARD. Don't apologize to me. Apologize to yourself. After all, you're the one who has insomnia. And I'll tell you of another who hasn't been sleeping properly; that's the one he actually did marry.

JANET (*after a pause; crossing below the table* RC *to the writing-table*) Do you ever think of the child?

LIBBARD. Hutton's child?

JANET. It's no joke to be the child of a criminal.

LIBBARD. It's no joke to be anybody's child; it's no joke to be born. And, anyhow, I'm still not convinced that Hutton is a criminal.

JANET (*picking up a pencil and doodling*) You mean, you don't think he was guilty? After all that came out at the trial?

LIBBARD. I've just been reading a very interesting book. It's an analysis of well-known cases of people who were condemned for crimes they never committed.

JANET. But they *proved* it.

LIBBARD. They proved it in these other cases too. Sometimes it was nothing but the circumstantial evidence. It all pointed to one conclusion. And, yet, that conclusion was wrong. But, it's rare when that happens. More often it's a combination of misleading circumstantial evidence and deliberate false witness.

JANET (*throwing down the pencil and turning*) Do you mean that somebody was telling lies?

LIBBARD. I don't know. I just can't believe that Hutton was responsible.

JANET. Then—then who was?

LIBBARD. What about Emily herself?

JANET. Emily? No, Emily wouldn't have committed suicide. She wasn't that sort of person.

LIBBARD. Yes, I must say, I was a bit surprised when you said that at the trial. She often talked to me about being tired of life —wanting to put an end to it all.

JANET. I never heard her talk that way. Never.

LIBBARD. Nor did Nurse Braddock, if I remember rightly.

JANET. I don't know what she said. And I don't care.

LIBBARD. Hutton cared all right. It carried a lot of weight with the jury. (*He rises and crosses to* R *of Janet*) Somebody who'd been with Emily, day and night, for the best part of two years. And she says she's never heard her so much as a whisper of suicide. And suicide was the main line of defence.

JANET. I'm not interested in lines of defence. I'm interested in the truth. I'm interested in justice. (*Her voice rises as she speaks, till it almost goes out of control*) If you're accusing me of telling lies, just because I hated that beast . . . (*She suddenly checks herself*) Why do you let me go on like this? Why don't you stop me?

LIBBARD. People don't like being stopped as a rule.

JANET. I don't really mean it. (*She crosses above Libbard to the fireplace*) It's just that I get worked up and then it seems to go on by itself. Do you know that awful feeling? (*She moves to the armchair down* R) As though you were a violin, and somebody were screwing up the strings—tighter and tighter. Oh, God! I wish it were all over. (*She sits*)

LIBBARD. All over? (*He crosses to the fireplace*) You seem to think this business is like something in the movies, or in a novel—you seem to think it has an *ending*. At eight o'clock next Friday morning, to be precise. But that won't be the finish.

JANET. What do you mean?

LIBBARD. Surely, it's obvious. In real life there aren't any endings. Only transitions, only a succession of new beginnings. (*He sits in the armchair above the fireplace*) Hutton's going to be hanged. But don't imagine you're going to be free of him. In one way or another this thing is going on. All you can do is to decide whether it shall go on in the worst possible way, or in some other way.

JANET. What other way?

LIBBARD. Ask yourself. All *I* know is that the way that's being followed now is the worst way. You can't sleep. And Hutton's going to be hanged for something he never did.

JANET. But it was proved.

LIBBARD. Not to my satisfaction.

JANET. It's nonsense to say it was suicide. Nurse Braddock never heard her say anything, I never heard her say anything. How could it have been?

LIBBARD. Very well, let's assume you're right.

JANET. I know I'm right.

LIBBARD. You know it wasn't Emily and I know it wasn't Hutton. Well, then, it must have come through some other agency.

JANET. I don't know what you're driving at.

LIBBARD. I'm driving at some way to make you sleep. (*He rises*) You can't sleep because somebody is sitting inside your head screwing up the strings. All right, get rid of that somebody. Open the door and show him out. (*He sits on the fender*) Then the strings will slacken again.

JANET. All these mixed metaphors—strings and doors and throwing people out. Why so poetical all of a sudden?

LIBBARD (*after a pause; rising and crossing to the writing-table*) Of course, you know the basic reason why poor Emily was so dreadfully unhappy?

JANET. What was that?

LIBBARD. It was because she wouldn't accept the facts as she found them. She was an invalid and she'd lost her looks. (*He picks up the doodle*) But she wanted people to treat her as though she were young and pretty. Hence all the misery.

(*There is a pause*)

JANET. What has that got to do with me?

LIBBARD. Nothing. I'm just pointing out that people can come to terms with even the most terrible facts. But they've got to accept them. They've got to adapt themselves to reality. (*He sits on the* R *end of the writing-table*)

JANET. Those are just words, that's all.

LIBBARD. No, they're more than that. I've known plenty of people who came to terms with death—even with pain, which is a good deal worse.

JANET (*after a pause*) Do you suppose Henry has come to terms with—with what's happening to him?

LIBBARD. I know he hasn't.

JANET. Up till now he's always been able to buy his way out of any trouble he got into. Not this time.

LIBBARD. You're quite right. And that's why it's so hard for him. And yet, it's always in our power to come to terms with the thing. And the quicker we come to terms, the better.

JANET. The better for whom?

LIBBARD (*rising*) For everybody concerned. And, especially ourselves, Janet. (*He moves* C)

JANET (*rising and moving* R *of Libbard*) Well, we've had a very interesting talk, Dr Libbard. Now, what about those sleeping tablets? Were you going to give me something a little stronger than you did last time?

(LIBBARD *looks at her for a moment, then shakes his head and sighs*)

LIBBARD. Well, if that's what you really want, I suppose you'd better have it. (*He moves to the writing-table, takes a prescription pad from his pocket, sits, and fills in a form*)

(JANET *eases to the fireplace*)

(*He looks up*) Janet, do you remember that young Dr Farjeon you met at my house last year?

JANET. Yes.

LIBBARD. I've known him ever since he was a boy. A very nice fellow—kind, sensible, conscientious.

JANET. No, thanks. I don't want to go to a psychiatrist.

LIBBARD. But you want to get well, don't you?

JANET. I'm not ill—not that way, anyhow. (*With sudden violence*) You're plotting to get me locked up. That's what it is.

LIBBARD. Now, Janet, don't talk nonsense. Nobody's plotting anything.

JANET. You think I'm mad. But it's true. You're trying to send me to a doctor for mad people. I tell you, there's nothing wrong with me. I just can't sleep, that's all.

LIBBARD. He can make you sleep, if you want him to.

JANET (*horrified*) Do you mean he'll hypnotize me?

LIBBARD. Well, what's so alarming about that?

JANET. Send me to sleep and then make me say all sorts of

things I don't want to say—and I shan't know I've said them. No, no, I won't. (*She crosses to R of the writing-table*) I know what you're up to, you and your hypnotist. Trying to get things out of me. Trying to drive me out of my mind so that you can have an excuse to lock me up. (*She snatches at the doodle*)

LIBBARD (*rising*) Listen, Janet. Be reasonable. (*He takes her hands*)

JANET (*quickly withdrawing her hands*) Don't touch me. I'm not a fool. I can see what you're trying to do.

LIBBARD. Janet . . . (*He lays a hand on her arm*)

(JANET *strikes savagely at his wrist*)

JANET. I'll kill you. (*She pauses*) Do you understand? (*She breaks to the fireplace*)

(*The front door bell rings. There is a pause, then* LIBBARD *shrugs his shoulders, turns, sits at the writing-table and resumes writing. The* MAID *enters up* L)

MAID. Mrs Hutton to see you, miss.

JANET (*nodding*) All right. Show her in. (*She sits on the fender, facing down* R)

MAID. Yes, miss.

(*The* MAID *exits up* L.
After a few moments DORIS *enters up* L. *She is dressed in her outdoor clothes and her fur coat conceals the fact that she is already far gone in pregnancy. Her face is very pale and she has evidently been crying.* LIBBARD *tears off the prescription form, puts it on the desk, replaces the pad in his pocket and rises*)

LIBBARD. Have you been all right?

(DORIS *nods*)

DORIS (*moving* C) I—I hope you don't mind my coming, Janet.

JANET (*without turning round*) Not a bit; I'm delighted.

LIBBARD (*moving* L *of Doris*) You went to see him today, didn't you?

DORIS. Yes, I went this morning. (*She pauses*) Oh, Dr Libbard, it was so terrible. (*She starts to cry*) His hands were all bleeding.

LIBBARD. Bleeding?

DORIS. From beating on the door. He wants them to let him talk to the governor of the prison. As if that would do any good. How can they do it, Dr Libbard? How can they kill a man who isn't guilty? You don't believe he's guilty, do you?

LIBBARD. You know I don't.

DORIS. And, meanwhile, they torture him. They keep him locked up there. They tell him when it's going to happen. And that awful clock keeps striking and striking till he's ready to go mad. (*She sobs*)

LIBBARD (*patting Doris's shoulder*) There, you can cry now. But I hope you didn't do it when you were with him.

DORIS. No, I remembered what you said. I did my best not to show what I was feeling. But I don't think it made any difference to him. I don't think anything would make any difference to him now. He can't think of anything but—but what's going to happen to him. Everything else is meaningless; it just doesn't exist. Even me, even the baby. And yet, before the appeal was rejected, he cared so much. It was so wonderful—as though we'd never loved one another before. And now it's all gone. There's nothing left except the clock and this awful thing that's coming nearer and nearer. (*She turns to Janet*) Janet, I know you think he's guilty.

JANET (*rising*) They proved it, didn't they?

DORIS. They proved it. And yet I swear he didn't do it. I *know* he didn't.

JANET. How do you expect me to go against the evidence?

DORIS. That's just what I came to talk to you about, Janet. You used to be his friend. You could still help him.

JANET. Me?

DORIS. You used to like him.

JANET. What's that got to do with the evidence?

DORIS. If you could just go and tell them it was a mistake.

JANET. A mistake? What was a mistake?

DORIS. About her never saying that she wanted to kill herself. If you told them you hadn't really meant it.

JANET. I did mean it. It's absolutely true.

DORIS. But, Janet . . .

JANET. I don't care what other people say. I never heard her talk that way. Never.

DORIS. But if other people heard her, then it means that it's true. So, it wouldn't be a lie. You could go and tell them that, after all, she did talk about it sometimes. They'd believe you, Janet; they'd do something. They might put it off—even now. Oh, Janet, please, please. (*She takes Janet's hand*)

(LIBBARD *eases down* L)

JANET (*snatching her hand away and moving down* R) Pawing and slobbering. Like dogs, like monkeys. (*She rubs her hand*) And then calling it love. (*She shudders*) And now he sends you to come and whine for mercy.

DORIS. He didn't send me. I came on my own.

JANET (*turning and crossing Doris to* L *of her*) Oh, she came on her own, did she? His whore, the little five-shilling whore he lost his head about. The sweet little baby whore who doesn't know anything about art or literature. But she knows a great deal about certain other things. Everything there is to be known. Kissing and . . .

LIBBARD. Janet!

JANET (*turning to Libbard*) That's it! Stand up for her. You'd like to do a little pawing and slobbering yourself, wouldn't you? And, meanwhile, I'm to go and say I told a lie. So that you can go on with your filthy love making.

DORIS. Janet, how can you?

JANET. You couldn't wait. You never even gave yourself a chance to find out what real love was like. Pawing and slobbering —that's all you cared about. So that you can mother the child of a criminal, the child of a man who's been hanged. Because that's what he's going to be—hanged, hanged by the neck until he is dead.

(*She strikes Doris on the face, stands for a moment staring at her, then suddenly covers her face with her hands, turns, runs up* L *and exits.*
As she reaches the arch, the LIGHTS *go out and the* L *gauze is drawn across. Simultaneously the* R *gauze is drawn aside and the* LIGHTS *go up on the Prison Cell*)

SCENE 2

SCENE—*The Prison Cell. The following afternoon.*

When the LIGHTS *come up,* HUTTON *is standing with his back to the audience, beating with his fists on the cell door up* C. *A* WARDER *can be seen through the grille.*

HUTTON (*beating on the door and calling*) Listen. For God's sake. I tell you, I'm innocent. I didn't do it. I swear I didn't. Let me talk to the Governor. Just for five minutes. I can explain everything. Please, please. He'll understand, if only you'll let me talk to him. It's all a mistake.

(*The* WARDER *moves away, and, as the sound of his footsteps diminishes,* HUTTON'S *voice rises in pitch and intensity, until he is almost screaming*)

No, don't go. I beg you. It's not right. It isn't justice. You can't let an innocent man be killed. Stop—for God's sake. Come back. (*He pauses and listens*) Come back. (*He raises his hands to rest on the door, then lets them drop with a gesture of despair. He turns and lies down on the edge of the bed and covers his face with his hands*)

(*The door is quietly opened and the* WARDER *admits* LIBBARD, *who enters and lays a hand on Hutton's shoulder.* HUTTON *starts and looks up. The* WARDER *closes the door and remains outside looking through the grille*)

Oh—oh, it's you. (*He sits up and seizes Libbard's arm*) Help me, Libbard, help me. For God's sake.

LIBBARD. I can only help you against yourself.

HUTTON. What do you mean?

LIBBARD. I can prevent you from torturing yourself, that's all.

HUTTON. But, Libbard, it's only two days now. Less than two days. Only a little more than forty hours. Forty hours . . .

LIBBARD. Well, that's time enough to be reconciled, time enough to come to terms with the facts. Look at your hands.

(HUTTON's *hands are still clutched around Libbard's arm*)

That's how you're holding on to yourself. And the tighter you hold, the more it hurts. Now, loosen your fingers. Loosen them.

(HUTTON *loosens his grip*)

Good. Now, let your hands drop on to your knees. Let them fall as though they didn't belong to you. Let them fall.

(HUTTON *allows his hands to fall palm upward into his lap*)

There, that's better. I've been trying to cure sick people for the last thirty-odd years and, I can tell you, most illnesses come from not being able to let go.

HUTTON (*rising and breaking down* L) But I'm not ill. I'm well. I'm perfectly well. (*He moves to Libbard and seizes his left arm*) And in two days they're going to kill me, they're going to . . .

LIBBARD. Listen to yourself. Do you think a man who talks like that is perfectly well?

(*The prison clock in the distance chimes three-quarters*)

HUTTON. That clock! (*He releases Libbard's arm, turns to the chair below the table and sits facing up stage*)

LIBBARD. Yes, the hands move forward; and the earth turns away from the sun; and soon the night will come, and then the morning, and then another night—and another morning. And there's nothing anybody can do about it. Nothing whatever. Well, is that any reason for turning the last two days of your life into a hell of fear and bitterness and resentment? Let go, I tell you, let go.

HUTTON (*after a long pause*) You've seen a lot of people die, haven't you?

LIBBARD. A great many.

HUTTON. Is it—is it very bad?

LIBBARD. The bad time is before—and it's bad only for the people who won't accept what's happening to them. They resist, they hold on. But the whole force of destiny is pushing them. All the screaming and struggling and hanging on—it's all perfectly useless. They just suffer a great deal unnecessarily—that's all. (*He moves the chair from above the table to* C *and sits*) It's a question of accepting what can't be avoided or escaped. And not only accepting it; actually willing it. "This is the inevitable, this is my destiny; and I *will* that it shall be exactly as it is." And when you say that, your destiny is right and good—however cruel it may have seemed to you before. The inevitable becomes the tolerable and even, in a certain sense, the reasonable.

HUTTON (*rising*) Reasonable? (*He crosses to* R)

LIBBARD. Yes, even this nightmare that you've had to live through. Even this . . .

HUTTON (*turning*) Libbard, I didn't do it. Do you believe me?

LIBBARD. I believe you.

HUTTON. And you still think that what's happened is reasonable?

LIBBARD. Not by our everyday standards. But when the thing can be accepted and willed, then there are other standards.

HUTTON. Do *you* accept it and will it?

LIBBARD. No, of course not. I can't accept a wrong which is being done to someone else, just as I can't accept to do wrong myself. In both cases I've got to do everything in my power to right the wrong. But a wrong that's inflicted on me, an evil that I suffer—those I *can* accept. And if I do accept them, if I go further and actually will them, then the wrong and the evil change their nature—change it so far as *I'm* concerned. Not so far as anyone else is concerned.

HUTTON. You mean, even injustice can become justice.

LIBBARD. For the victim. Not for the judge or the spectator.

HUTTON (*sitting on the bed*) Of course, in a way all this isn't entirely unjust. I didn't kill Emily—but I certainly tortured her. I knew how unhappy she was and I accepted her suffering, I willed it. And I went on willing it, because I wasn't prepared to forgo my amusements. It's terrible what monstrous things one's ready to do, just to amuse oneself. It all seemed so trivial and excusable at the time. But now, now I know better—and it's too late.

LIBBARD. It's never too late to recognize the truth.

HUTTON (*after a pause*) Do you think we all get what we deserve?

LIBBARD. What else do we get? God is not mocked: as a man sows, so shall he reap.

HUTTON (*rising and moving to* R *of the door*) And yet I don't believe I'm any worse than plenty of other men I know. And what are *they* doing at this moment? Shooting pheasants, or telephoning to their stockbrokers, or dozing in an armchair at the club.

LIBBARD. You're talking like the *Book of Job*. As though good men ought always to be rich and healthy, and bad men always poor and covered with carbuncles. But that's just childish.

(HUTTON *breaks down* R)

Shooting pheasants and telephoning to one's stockbroker aren't necessarily the rewards of virtue. On the contrary, they may be punishments. After all, a man who spends his time on that sort of thing isn't spending it on anything else. Which means that he's some sort of a spiritual abortion. And being an abortion, when you might be a fully developed human being—what's that but the most terrible of punishments?

(HUTTON *sits on the bed*)

Whereas being poor, or sick, or even being unjustly condemned, yes, even that—all these may be actually rewarding situations. Mind you, they aren't necessarily so. Far from it. But they *may* be; that is, if you react to them in the right way.

HUTTON. And yet most of us would rather lead a normal, sensual life.

LIBBARD. Of course. It's so much easier—and lazier. But to grow into a fully-developed human being is always much more rewarding—however painful the process of growth may be.

HUTTON. And yet if you do accept the responsibilities there's an extraordinary satisfaction. I was just discovering that with Doris. Of course you know how it began. In wantonness as a kind of joke. Deliberately shutting my eyes to what she really was in herself and thinking only of what I could get out of her, which was simply a kind of intoxication. The pleasure of dominating another human being through sensuality and the pleasure of annihilating one's own self, of taking a holiday from one's humanity. It only changed after she tried to kill herself. Suddenly I saw her as a real person. A real person whom I had treated as a thing—and very nearly destroyed. All through the trial I kept thinking of the time when one could go forward in that new relationship. But now . . .

LIBBARD. But if you accept the facts, if you will them.

HUTTON. Yes, the pain doesn't seem to be quite so bad. Perhaps I could think of her for a change.

LIBBARD. She's coming again tomorrow.

HUTTON. One human being saying good-bye to another human being. It has a value, it makes some kind of sense.

WARDER (*through the grille*) Time's up, sir. (*He opens the door*)

(LIBBARD *rises, lays his hand on Hutton's shoulder for a moment, then turns and exits.*

The WARDER *closes the door.* HUTTON *half rises, then sits again on the bed and for a few moments stares at the floor. As he lifts his head to the window the prison clock in the distance chimes the hour of five. He collapses on the bed. As he does so, the* LIGHTS *go out and the* R *gauze is drawn across. Simultaneously the* L *gauze is drawn aside and the* LIGHTS *go up on the Spences' room* L)

Scene 3

SCENE—*The Spences' living-room. Late the following night.*

When the LIGHTS *go up, the clock shows the time to be approximately one forty-five. The curtains are drawn, the fire is burning and the lamp on the mantelpiece is lit. The armchair from above the fireplace is now* L *of the table* RC *on which a chessboard and chessmen are spread. The* GENERAL *is asleep in his wheelchair in the corner up* R. JANET, *seated on the fender, is poring over a volume of the Encyclopaedia. Several other thick reference books lay scattered on the floor. The* NURSE *is standing* C, *knitting. There is a long pause, then the Nurse moves to Janet and speaks in her most brightly professional manner.*

NURSE. It's getting awfully late, Miss Spence. Don't you think you ought to toddle off to bed?

JANET. I've told you, I'm not going to bed. Not till—not till after eight o'clock tomorrow morning. When's Dr Libbard coming?

NURSE. All he said was that it'd be very late. He had an urgent case to attend to some miles away.

JANET. I don't know why you ever sent for him. *I* don't need him.

NURSE. Well, your father wanted it. He's worried about you, my dear. Now, Miss Spence, let me help you to bed, and then I'll bring you a nice glass of hot milk. And perhaps when Dr Libbard comes he'll give you something that'll really send you to sleep.

JANET. Oh no! I'm not going to sleep till I know it's all right for me to sleep. I'm not a fool.

NURSE (*putting her knitting on the mantelpiece*) Come along, dear. There's a good girl. (*She lays a hand on Janet's shoulder*)

JANET (*violently*) Don't touch me. (*She rises, closes her book, puts it on the fender, then moves to the armchair down* R *and sits*)

(*The* GENERAL *stirs*)

NURSE (*turning*) Yes, General? (*To Janet*) He's still asleep. (*She picks up a book from the floor, and crosses to the writing-table*) All these Encyclopaedias. (*She opens the book*) They're such small print. You'll ruin your eyes.

JANET (*rising and crossing to* R *of the Nurse*) What are you doing with that?

NURSE. Just improving my mind, that's all. Adult education— isn't that what they call it?

JANET (*snatching the volume out of the Nurse's hand*) You're trying to spy on me. (*She throws the book on the writing-table*)

NURSE. Spy on you?

JANET (*crossing to the fireplace*) I tell you, you'd better be careful. I know your tricks. You're working with Libbard.

NURSE. But, Miss Spence . . .
JANET (*picking up her book off the fender*) Go away.

(*The front door bell rings.* JANET *sits on the fender and resumes reading her book. The* GENERAL *wakes up*)

GENERAL. What's that? What is it, Nurse?
NURSE. It's all right, General, that's Dr Libbard. I'll go and let him in.

(*The* NURSE *exits up* L.
JANET *becomes deeply absorbed in her book. There is a pause, then the* GENERAL *moves himself in his wheelchair to* L *of the armchair* C)

GENERAL. Janet.

(JANET *does not look up*)

(*Louder*) Janet.
JANET (*starting*) What is it, Father?
GENERAL. I want you to promise me something.
JANET (*suspiciously*) Oh—it depends what it is.
GENERAL. No, promise first.
JANET (*putting her book on the fender*) Well, I suppose I can trust you. (*She rises*)
GENERAL. Take a rest, take a good holiday.

(JANET *kneels on the floor above the table and looks at the chessmen*)

You haven't been away for months and months. I don't need you. I've got this damned woman here. So don't think about me. Go abroad. Get away from it all.
JANET. Get away from it all.
GENERAL. After all, Emily's dead. Worrying won't bring her back. What's the good of it?
JANET (*playing with the chessmen*) Sometimes one can't help doing a thing—even when it isn't any good.
GENERAL. Don't I know it? (*He holds out his hand, which trembles violently*) What's the good of that? Spill the soup, that's all. But I can't help it. And what's the good of *me*, if it comes to that? So carry on as if I weren't here. Go away. Have a spree.
JANET (*smiling*) I'll have a spree.
GENERAL. And damn the expense. None of your Swiss *pensions*. Good hotels, decent restaurants. I'll give you the money. Free as a bird. Start tomorrow, if you want to.
JANET. Tomorrow.
GENERAL. And pick up a husband while you're about it.

(JANET *sweeps the chessmen off the board on to the floor*)

Janet! Janet!

(LIBBARD *enters up* L)

C

LIBBARD (*moving above the armchair* C) Good evening, Janet.

JANET (*without looking up; coldly*) Good evening. (*She rises and moves to the fireplace*)

LIBBARD (*to the General*) Oughtn't you to be in bed by this time, General?

(*The* NURSE *enters up* L)

GENERAL (*turning his chair to face up stage*) Didn't want to leave the girl alone. She's ill. Ought to have a rest. Ought to have a complete change.

LIBBARD. You're right. I'll see what I can do. Nurse, I think you'd better take the General to his room.

NURSE. Very well, Doctor.

GENERAL (*wheeling himself off up* L) Don't let it get you down, my girl. And afterwards, remember—a good spree. Good night, Doctor.

(*The* GENERAL *exits up* L)

LIBBARD. Good night. You understand, Nurse?

NURSE. Yes, Dr Libbard. (*As she goes*) Now come along, General, we'll soon get you to bed.

(*The* NURSE *exits up* L)

JANET. What does she understand?

LIBBARD. I thought perhaps you might like something later on to make you sleep. I've told Nurse Braddock what to do.

JANET. I suppose you'd like to put me to sleep.

LIBBARD. Well, I'd like at least to persuade you to go to bed, for everybody's sake.

JANET. Doctor's orders?

LIBBARD. Just a friendly suggestion.

JANET (*crossing below the table to the arch*) Why not? One should only stay up for things of importance.

(JANET *turns and exits up* L.

LIBBARD *stands a moment, then moves to the arch and glances off. He then moves quickly to the clock up* R, *opens the front and advances the hands to almost three o'clock. He again moves to the arch, switches off the lights, leaving the room only illuminated by the table-lamp on the mantelpiece, crosses to the alcove, selects a book, moves to the armchair down* R *and sits. He takes his watch from his pocket and alters it, then opens the book and starts to read.*

There is a long pause, then JANET *enters up* L, *switches on the lights and moves down* L)

Still here? I hoped you'd be gone. I don't know what you ever came for.

LIBBARD. Well, it's a pretty unpleasant occasion. I thought perhaps . . .

(*The clock strikes three*)

JANET. It's late. (*She turns the chair down* L *to face* R *and sits look-ing at the clock*)   Five hours more. (*She pauses*) Do people ever die of fear?

LIBBARD. I suppose it could happen. But of course the heart would have to be in pretty bad shape.

JANET. These idiotic Encyclopaedias. They never tell one the things one really wants to know.

LIBBARD. Such as?

JANET (*leaning towards him*)   When a man's hanged, how long does it take before he's dead?

LIBBARD (*matter-of-factly; without showing any surprise*)   Well, it depends. If you just put a noose round his neck and let him strangle under his own weight, he mightn't die for five or ten minutes.

JANET (*whispering*)   Five or ten minutes? (*She is silent for a moment, then utters a strange little grunt of laughter*)

LIBBARD. Nowadays, of course, they don't do it like that. They let the man drop eight or ten feet before the rope tightens. The shock breaks his neck.

JANET (*after a pause*)   Do you think he deserves to die so easily?

LIBBARD. I don't think he deserves to die at all.

JANET. I know why you said that. Just to get me angry. It's part of your little scheme.

LIBBARD. What scheme?

JANET. Trying to make me lose my head. Then I'll say things I don't mean to say. But this time I'm not going to oblige. You can talk about him as much as you like; *I* shan't say anything.

(*There is a pause*)

LIBBARD. It would still be possible to do it. (*He looks at his watch*)

JANET. To do what?

LIBBARD. To have the execution postponed.

JANET. Why should it be postponed?

LIBBARD. If some entirely new fact were to turn up.

JANET. Are you trying to get me to do what Doris wanted? I tell you, she didn't threaten to kill herself.

LIBBARD. She did. But I don't think she carried out the threat.

JANET. No, of course not. She was killed.

LIBBARD. But not by Hutton.

JANET. They proved it.

LIBBARD. The jury thought that they proved it. But do you?

(JANET *stares at Libbard without answering*)

Think it over, Janet. (*He rises and moves to the fireplace*) Of course, I can quite understand your not wanting to go to sleep until you feel you're safe. But did you ever stop to analyse the word? Safe

C*

from what? Safe in which respect? You can shut the door against one danger, and be wide open to another. Safe from death, for example, and safe from going mad under the fear of death. But does that mean you're safe from going mad because you've refused to face the danger of death, because you feel guilty for having refused? And does that mean that you won't be tempted, in the misery of your madness, to do away with yourself? But, that's death again. You run away from death and madness. But, what do you run into? Madness and death.

JANET (*rising*) Well, I'll think about it. I'm terribly thirsty. Would you like a drink?

LIBBARD. Yes, that's not a bad idea.

(JANET *crosses to the cabinet up* R. *While she is busy with the glasses and the bottles,* LIBBARD *stands with an elbow on the mantelpiece, looking at a bronze Indian figure*)

Kali, isn't it? The Great Mother. And precisely because she's the mother, she's also the goddess of destruction.

(JANET, *with her back to the audience, pours out two drinks*)

Not too much whisky, by the way. Just a *chota* peg, as your father would say.

JANET (*over her shoulder*) Just a *chota* peg.

LIBBARD. If you give life, you must also give death, inevitably.

JANET (*turning and moving to Libbard with a glass in each hand*) Here you are. (*She hands one glass to Libbard*)

LIBBARD (*taking the glass*) Thanks. (*He places it on the downstage end of the mantelpiece*) I must say they had a pretty realistic view of the world, those old Hindus. (*He deliberately knocks the glass on to the floor*)

(JANET *utters a cry*)

LIBBARD. Clumsy of me! I'm really awfully sorry. However, I don't think it'll do any harm to the carpet, do you? Just a little fizzy water and a spot of alcohol, that's all. Am I allowed another glass?

JANET (*turning*) Let me get it for you.

LIBBARD (*moving to the cabinet*) Don't bother. (*He pours himself another drink*)

(JANET *moves to the chair down* L)

(*He turns and raises his glass*) To your better health. (*He drinks*)

(JANET *sits. For a few seconds she looks at Libbard in silence then starts to laugh. As she does so, the* LIGHTS *go out and the* L *gauze is drawn across. Simultaneously the* R *gauze is drawn aside and the* LIGHTS *go up on the prison cell* R)

Scene 4

Scene—*The Prison Cell. The same night.*

When the Lights *go up* Hutton *is lying on the bed, reading, his head down stage. A* Warder *is standing* l *of the door, working at a crossword puzzle. There is silence for a few moments. The* Warder *scratches his head and frowns in perplexity.*

Warder (*to himself*) Mythical bird, mythical bird . . .
Hutton (*looking up from his book*) What's your trouble?
Warder. Mythical bird. Seven letters. Begins with "P".
Hutton. Begins with a "P"? What about "Phoenix"? P-H-O-E-N-I-X.
Warder. "Phoenix." That's it. (*He writes down the word*)
Hutton. Incidentally, it rose from the dead if that's of any interest to you. (*He pauses*) I came across something here—something extraordinary. Do you mind if I read it out to you?
Warder. No, no. Go ahead.
Hutton (*reading aloud; very slowly and distinctly*) "The difference between a good man and a bad man does not lie in this, that the one wills that which is good and the other does not, but solely in this, that the one concurs with the living, inspiring spirit of God within him, and the other resists it, and can be chargeable with evil only because he resists it." (*He closes the book and puts it on the bed*)
Warder (*sitting in the chair up* l) It's a bit too deep for me.
Hutton (*sitting up*) Deep, yes; but clear, crystal clear. Don't you see what a lot of things it explains? For example, why did Christ think that the scribes and Pharisees were worse than the publicans and sinners? And, remember who the scribes and Pharisees were—the good citizens, the presidents of the chambers of commerce, the members of parliament, the successful lawyers, the professors of theology—all the really sound, respectable people. And he regarded them as being worse, in some ways, than the scum of the earth. And, of course, if a bad man is bad simply because he shuts himself off from the spirit of God within him, then it's obvious why he thought like that about the scribes and Pharisees. They were all so busy doing the proper, conventional things and all so cocksure of being the benefactors of the human race that it was impossible for them even to be aware of the spirit of God within them—much less to concur with it. And when you're in that state, I suppose you're in hell, though you mayn't know it, of course—not at the moment; but later on, perhaps, somewhere else. God knows. (*He shrugs his shoulders, then smiles slightly to himself, closes his eyes, and quotes*)

"It is a party in a parlour,
    Crammed, just as they on earth were crammed,
    Some sipping punch, some sipping tea,
    And all as silent as could be,
    All silent, and all damned."

(*He opens his eyes and smiles at the Warder*) And if they'd been talking —talking the sort of stuff people usually talk at parties—the damnation would have been even more complete.

(*There is a pause, then the* WARDER *rises, takes a packet of cigarettes from his pocket and offers one to Hutton*)

WARDER. How are your hands?

HUTTON (*taking a cigarette*) Still a bit sore. But there won't be any more hammering on doors. Not now. And, by the way, I'd like to thank you for being as gentle with me as you were.

WARDER (*lighting Hutton's cigarette*) I'm sorry if I ever had to be rough or anything. It was all in the course of duty, you understand.

HUTTON. Well, it was nothing to what I've done in the course of *not* doing my duty. That's why I'm here, I suppose—for resisting the spirit of God within me; resisting it by means of lies, by means of lust, by means of insensitiveness towards other people, by means of every kind of selfishness. And, resisting it by being a rich, respected member of the ruling class.

WARDER. But those aren't crimes.

HUTTON. No, they're something more fundamental than crimes, something worse in a certain way. But yet they can't be punished by law. (*He pauses*) Life has to be lived forwards; but it can only be understood backwards. I suppose that's why we always make the important discoveries too late.

(*The* 2ND WARDER *appears outside the door*)

2ND WARDER (*off*) Don't pay any attention to us, ma'am.

(HUTTON *rises and gives his cigarette to the* 1ST WARDER *who picks up his cap and puts it on*)

Just carry on as if we weren't there. (*He opens the door*)

(DORIS *enters.*
    The 1ST WARDER *exits, closing the door behind him. The* 2ND WARDER *remains outside the door, visible through the grille.* DORIS *moves to* L *of* HUTTON *who lays his left hand on her right shoulder and looks at her intently at arm's length. Suddenly* DORIS's *feelings get the better of her; her eyes fill with tears, her expression changes to the distorted grimace of uncontrollable grief, and she hides her face against his left shoulder, sobbing.* HUTTON *strokes her hair in silence. After a few seconds she raises her head and starts to wipe her eyes*)

DORIS. I'm sorry. (*She pauses*) Oh, your poor hands.

Hutton. Yes, I treated them pretty badly, didn't I? (*He leads her to the chair down* l)

(Doris *sits*)

(*He moves the chair above the table to* c *and sits on it* r *of Doris*) It must have been lovely in the country. Have the leaves begun to turn yet?

Doris. Yes, everything's brown and red and golden.

Hutton. Even the beech trees?

(Doris *nods affirmatively*)

I remember when I was a little boy—in the beech-woods at Arundel—walking in the dry leaves. I used to pretend to myself that it was money—knee deep in gold, like Aladdin. (*He pauses*) There's a theory nowadays that you oughtn't to bring up children on fairy stories. Don't let them talk you into any of that nonsense. Promise.

Doris (*her voice breaking*) I promise.

Hutton. If it's Belinda, she'll probably prefer *Hans Andersen* to anything else. Personally, I always found him a bit too sad and sentimental. If Patrick's like me, he'll like the *Arabian Nights*. That and the *Rose and the Ring*. How I loved the *Rose and the Ring*! My father used to read it aloud to me about six times a year. (*He pauses*) I'm afraid that'll be *your* job.

Doris (*sobbing uncontrollably*) I wish I were dead, I wish I'd never been born.

Hutton. What's the good of wishing? We *have* been born. And if one comes here, one has got to be prepared to go away again.

(Doris *goes on sobbing*)

Darling, you mustn't grieve, you mustn't. I tell you, everything's all right. Even my being here. Even—even our having to say good-bye to one another. Yes, ultimately even that's all right. *I know* it is. And you can know it too.

Doris. I can't, I can't.

Hutton. I thought *I* couldn't, until two days ago. Did Libbard tell you he'd been to see me?

(Doris *nods*)

He helped me—he helped me a great deal. (*He rises and moves* r) All the same, after he'd gone—well, it was bad again. (*He sits on the bed*) It was like having a terrible physical pain; and it's so excruciating that you can't think of anything else. It's the only reality. And then, all at once, the pain stops and, for the first time since it started, you see that there's a sun in the sky, you realize that those shadows out there are real people, you discover that your own wretched body isn't the whole world; there's all the rest of the universe. (*He pauses*) Do you love me, Doris?

(DORIS *rises, moves to him and kneels with her head in his lap*)

And you believe that I love you?

DORIS. I know you do.

(HUTTON *places his hand on her head and lifts his head to the window. As he does so, the* LIGHTS *go out and the* R *gauze is drawn across. Simultaneously, the* L *gauze is drawn aside and the* LIGHTS *go up on Spences' living-room* L)

SCENE 5

SCENE—*The Spences' living-room. Early the next morning.*

When the LIGHTS *go up the clock shows the time to be five minutes to eight. It is already light, but the lights are still burning.* LIBBARD *and* JANET *are seated at the table* RC *playing beggar-my-neighbour.* JANET'S *manner has become strangely childish. She is greatly excited and keeps bursting into peals of laughter. She is sitting in the armchair from up* R, *which is now* L *of the table* RC. LIBBARD *is seated on the fender.*

JANET (*dealing out a card from her portion of the pack*) A king.

LIBBARD (*dealing out three cards*) One, two, queen of hearts.

JANET (*dealing*) One, ace of diamonds.

LIBBARD (*dealing*) One, two, three. I daren't look at the fourth. (*He turns it up*) Thank goodness! Another queen.

JANET. Let's see what *I* can do. (*She turns up a card*) Knave of clubs.

LIBBARD. Heavens! Well, here goes. (*He turns up a card*) Oh!

(JANET *laughs triumphantly and takes all the cards that have been dealt out into her hand*)

JANET. Mine, all mine. You're no good at all.

LIBBARD. I'm just not clever enough, that's the trouble. This is a game that takes intellect.

JANET. Ready?

(JANET *deals a card,* LIBBARD *does the same; this goes on through several exchanges until* JANET *turns up a court card*)

At last. The king of spades.

LIBBARD (*dealing*) One, two ... Heavens, that's the end. You've done for me.

(JANET *breaks out once more into delighted laughter*)

I owe you ten million pounds.

JANET. Eleven million.

LIBBARD (*rising*) Eleven is it? God help me! (*He moves to the window up* C, *draws the curtains and looks out*) It looks like rain.

JANET. I like rain. I like it when it rains really hard, when there's thunder and lightning . . . (*She suddenly breaks off, and her expression changes*) Oh, God! (*She puts her hands to her head, as though she had suddenly remembered something terrible*) God! (*She covers her face and shudders*) And that girl, that girl . . . Oh, it's too horrible. Like animals. I hate him, I hate him.

LIBBARD (*turning*) Do you know what the time is?

(JANET *looks at the clock. It marks two minutes to eight*)

JANET (*whispering*) Only two minutes.

LIBBARD. That's all. Two minutes. Then you'll be safe.

JANET (*rising*) I'll be safe. (*She pauses, facing down* R) They must have got everything ready on the scaffold. The rope, the straps. And there's the governor of the prison and the chaplain. They're walking along the corridor. It isn't far. Just a few steps. They're at the door. Somebody puts a key in the lock and turns it. The door opens and there he is. (*She pauses*) Just because she was twenty-two. Because of her mouth. Because of her skin.

(*The clock strikes eight*)

God, God, God! (*She collapses into the armchair* C)

LIBBARD (*moving above Janet's chair*) It's all right. You can go to sleep now. Let yourself go. Now you can sleep. You feel safe now, don't you?

JANET. Safe. (*She closes her eyes*)

LIBBARD. Nurse.

(*The* NURSE *enters up* L. *She is carrying a small tray on which there is a hypodermic syringe, a small bowl and some cotton wool.* LIBBARD *moves the chair from down* L *to* L *of Janet, sits and rolls up her left sleeve. The* NURSE *eases to* L *of Libbard*)

Tell me, Janet, how did you get her to take the poison? (*He takes a piece of cotton wool, dips it in the bowl and cleans the inside of Janet's forearm*)

JANET. I put it in the coffee.

LIBBARD. You thought he'd ask you to marry him? (*He puts the piece of cotton wool on the tray*)

(*The* NURSE *hands him the syringe*)

JANET. Yes. No.

LIBBARD. You thought he loved you? As much as you loved him?

JANET. It was too awful. Too humiliating. (*Her voice breaks*)

LIBBARD. It's all right. I won't torment you any more. Now this won't hurt. (*He makes the injection*) You can sleep now. Sleep. Just sleep. (*He replaces the syringe on the tray, takes another piece of cotton wool, wipes Janet's arm, then watches her intently for a few moments to make sure she is asleep*) Nurse—the telephone. (*He rises*)

(*The* NURSE *puts the tray on the writing-table and lifts the telephone receiver.* LIBBARD *moves to the clock up* R *and turns the hands back to seven o'clock, then moves* L *of Janet and lifts her eyelid for a moment*)

NURSE (*into the telephone*)   May I have that call for Dr Libbard now, please . . . Yes. Whitehall four-six-five-six . . . All right, I'll hold on.

(LIBBARD *moves above the* NURSE *to* L *of her and takes the telephone receiver from her. The* NURSE *turns and looks at Janet*)

LIBBARD (*into the telephone*)   Hullo, I want to speak to the Home Secretary . . . Yes, it's Dr James Libbard speaking. He is expecting me to call him before seven-thirty . . . Yes, that's right . . . Connected with the Hutton case. Extremely urgent . . . Thank you. I'll wait.

CURTAIN

FURNITURE AND PROPERTY PLOT

ACT I

SCENE 1

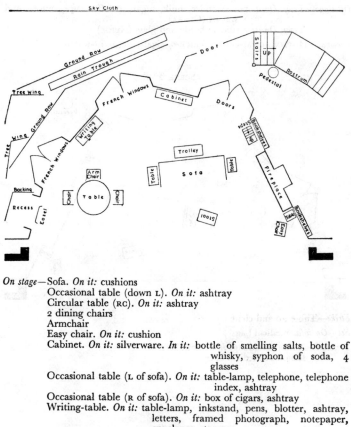

On stage—Sofa. *On it:* cushions
Occasional table (down L). *On it:* ashtray
Circular table (RC). *On it:* ashtray
2 dining chairs
Armchair
Easy chair. *On it:* cushion
Cabinet. *On it:* silverware. *In it:* bottle of smelling salts, bottle of whisky, syphon of soda, 4 glasses
Occasional table (L of sofa). *On it:* table-lamp, telephone, telephone index, ashtray
Occasional table (R of sofa). *On it:* box of cigars, ashtray
Writing-table. *On it:* table-lamp, inkstand, pens, blotter, ashtray, letters, framed photograph, notepaper, envelopes, stamps
Waste-paper basket
Library steps
Stool
Easel
Canvases (1 of a nude)
Fender
Fire-irons
Hearth rug

71

> *On mantelpiece:* clock, brass candlesticks
> *In bookshelves:* books
> *On walls:* Post-Impressionist French paintings
> 2 pairs of curtains
> Carpet on floor

Set—On table RC: bowl of fruit, 3 fruit plates, glass of water, 1 spoon, 1 fork, 3 wine glasses, 2 fruit knives, decanter of wine, cloth
> *Above sofa:* trolley. *On it:* dish of red-currants (*stewed*), 2 plates, serving spoon
> *Outside window up* C: large tin

*Off stage—*Tray. *On it:* pot of coffee, milk, sugar, 4 coffee cups, saucers and spoons (CLARA)
> Tray. *On it:* medicine bottle and glass (NURSE)

*Personal—*HUTTON: cigar-cutter, matches, cigar-case, wrist-watch

SCENE 2

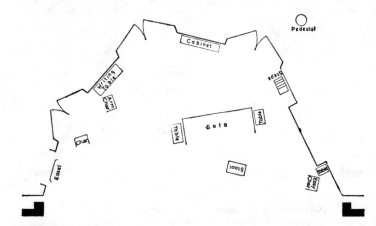

*Strike—*Table RC and chair L of it

Set—On sofa: medical bag

*Personal—*NURSE: handbag. *In it:* handkerchief
> LIBBARD: medical bag

ACT II

SCENE 1

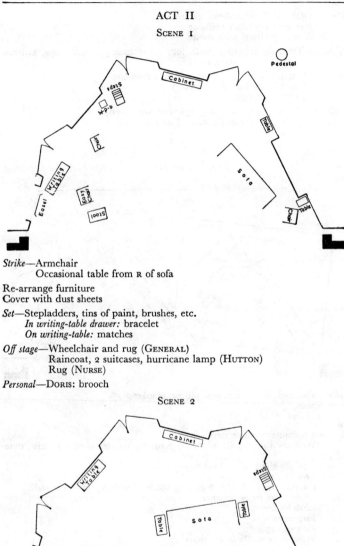

Strike—Armchair
   Occasional table from R of sofa

Re-arrange furniture
Cover with dust sheets

Set—Stepladders, tins of paint, brushes, etc.
   In writing-table drawer: bracelet
   On writing-table: matches

Off stage—Wheelchair and rug (GENERAL)
   Raincoat, 2 suitcases, hurricane lamp (HUTTON)
   Rug (NURSE)

Personal—DORIS: brooch

SCENE 2

Strike—Stepladders, paint pots, dust sheets, brushes, easel
Re-arrange furniture

Set—*On sofa:* child's teddy-bear, eiderdown
　　On floor down L: child's golliwog
　　In alcove R: pedestal with statue

Off stage—Tray. *On it:* teapot, milk jug, sugar basin, 2 each cups, saucers,
　　　　　　spoons

Personal—DORIS: watch, handbag. *In it:* handkerchief
　　　　　　NURSE: handbag. *In it:* tablets
　　　　　　JANET: handbag

During Black-Out set—*On table* R *of sofa:* hot-water bottle
　　　　　　　　　　On writing-table: LIBBARD'S *bag*

ACT III

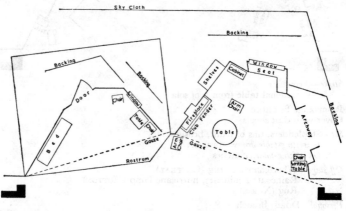

Cell—Pallet bed. *On it:* mattress, pillow, blanket
　　　Table
　　　2 chairs

Room—2 upholstered armchairs
　　　Writing-table. *On it:* inkstand, pens, blotter, telephone, pencils, note-
　　　　　　　　paper
　　　Upright chair
　　　Low table
　　　Cabinet. *On it:* books, 3 glasses, bottle of whisky, syphon of soda
　　　　　　In it: ornaments
　　　Club fender
　　　Fire-irons
　　　Hearth rug
　　　Window-seat. *On it:* cushions
　　　Alcove shelves. *On them:* statues of Krishna and Buddha, books, papers,
　　　　　　　　tin of dog biscuits, bottle of medicine, glass, chess-
　　　　　　　　board, chessmen, pack of playing cards
　　　Clock
　　　Indian hangings
　　　Oriental weapons
　　　On mantelpiece: statuette of Kali, table-lamp
　　　Curtains at window
　　　Carpet

SCENE I

Set clock at 4 o'clock
Off stage—Paper bag, rug (GENERAL)
Personal—JANET: bracelet
          LIBBARD: prescription pad

SCENE 2

During this scene prepare room
Re-set clock

Set—Encyclopaedia on fender
      Reference books on floor
      Armchair from above fireplace to C
      On table RC: Chessboard and chessmen

SCENE 3

Personal—NURSE: knitting
          LIBBARD: watch

During this scene set in cell—Warder's cap on table. Book on bed

SCENE 4

Personal—WARDER: newspaper open at crossword puzzle, pencil, packet of
                cigarettes, matches
          DORIS: handkerchief

During this scene—Clear chessboard, chessmen, and glass from floor
                Set on table RC: pack of cards
                Re-set clock

SCENE 5

Off stage—Tray. *On it:* hypodermic syringe, small bowl, cotton wool (NURSE)

LIGHTING PLOT

ACT I SCENE 1 Midday
All lights full up
No cues

ACT I SCENE 2 Midnight
To open: All lights out

Cue 1	HUTTON switches on lamp L of sofa	(page 14)
	Lights up to ½	
Cue 2	HUTTON switches on lamp on writing-table	(page 18)
	Lights up to full	

ACT II SCENE 1 Evening
To open: All lights out

Cue 3	HUTTON switches on lamp L	(page 22)
	Lights up to ½	
Cue 4	JANET: ". . . tear them to pieces, destroy them."	(page 24)
	BLACK-OUT *except off-stage lighting*	
Cue 5	HUTTON lights hurricane lamp	(page 25)
	Lights up to ¼	
Cue 6	JANET: "Oh, nothing in particular."	(page 28)
	Lights up to ¾	
Cue 7	HUTTON blows out lamp	(page 28)
	Lights down to ½	

ACT II SCENE 2 Afternoon
To open: All lights full up

Cue 8	DORIS takes tablets	(page 43)
	Quick fade to BLACK-OUT	
Cue 9	CURTAIN rises	(page 43)
	Quick rise to ½, bringing in table-lamp L	

ACT III
To open: Lights on both sets well dimmed

ACT III SCENE 1 Afternoon

Cue 10	HUTTON looks up	(page 48)
	BLACK-OUT R. *Lights full up on* L	
Cue 11	JANET exits	(page 56)
	BLACK-OUT L. *Lights full up on* R	

ACT III SCENE 2

Cue 12	HUTTON *looks up*	(page 59)
	BLACK-OUT R. *Lights up to ¾ on* L	

ACT III   SCENE 3   Night

Cue 13   LIBBARD switches off lights   (page 62)
         Lights down to ¼

Cue 14   JANET switches on lights   (page 62)
         Lights up to ¾

Cue 15   JANET laughs   (page 64)
         BLACK-OUT L. *Lights full up on* R

ACT III   SCENE 4

Cue 16   HUTTON looks up   (page 68)
         BLACK-OUT R. *Lights up to ¾ on* L

ACT III   SCENE 5   Morning

Cue 17   LIBBARD opens curtains   (page 68)
         Lights up to full

THUNDER PLOT

(ACT II, SCENE I)

Cue 1   JANET: "Of course not."
Cue 2   HUTTON: ". . . in town for a bit."
Cue 3   HUTTON: "Just a few feet away from me."
Cue 4   JANET: ". . . tear them to pieces, destroy them."
Cue 5   JANET: "One, two, three . . ."
Cue 6   HUTTON: ". . . too close for my taste."
Cue 7   HUTTON: ". . . mention friends and even . . ."
Cue 8   JANET: "She could only . . ."
Cue 9   HUTTON: ". . . got an umbrella."
Cue 10   HUTTON: ". . . you don't understand."

LIGHTNING

Cue 1   JANET: ". . . going to be away, Henry?"
Cue 2   JANET: "I love thunderstorms, don't you?"
Cue 3   JANET: ". . . they're tied down."
Cue 4   HUTTON: ". . . in seeing the lighting."
Cue 5   JANET: ". . . against all your feelings."
Cue 6   HUTTON: "Health, money, books . . ."
Cue 7   JANET: ". . . tastes and interests."
Cue 8   JANET: ". . . wind and the rain."
Cue 9   HUTTON: "It's impossible."

MADE AND PRINTED IN GREAT BRITAIN BY
BUTLER & TANNER LTD, FROME AND LONDON
MADE IN ENGLAND